CARNIVOROUS
CRICKETS
OF
COLORADO

Here's what readers from around the country are saying about Johnathan Rand's AMERICAN CHILLERS:

"I have read every single one of your books, and they are all AWESOME!"

-Ashley Y., age 12, California

"Thank you so much for coming to our school! The assembly was funny! I thought you were going to be really scary, but you weren't."

-Aaron P., age 11, Ohio

"I bought a pair of googly glasses from your website and I wear them everywhere. They are so cool!"

-James T., Age 8, Texas

"I just read VICIOUS VACUUMS OF VIRGINIA and it really creeped me out! It's my favorite book!"

-Samantha N., Age 11, Virginia

"Thank you so much for writing American Chillers. It's my favorite series in the whole world."

-Sean C., Age 9, Indiana

"My mom says the cover of DANGEROUS DOLLS OF DELAWARE really freaks her out. I read it and the story was even freakier than the cover!"

-Amber T., age 10, New York

"Our teacher read KREEPY KLOWNS OF KALAMAZOO to us, and it was great. Everyone in my class is in love with your books!"

-Payton K., Age 10, Michigan

"How come you always end every chapter at a good part? It drives me crazy because I have to keep reading to find out what happened!"

-Shannon L., Age 12, Colorado

"My family and I went to Chillermania and you were there with all three of your dogs! It was the best day of my life!"

-Michael R., Age 10, Michigan

"I just started reading your books and I love them! I'm going to read your whole series!"

-Sandra B., Age 9, Mississippi

"I read your books under the covers with a flashlight every night. They give me nightmares, but I love every book!"

-Robbie H., age 10, Oregon

"I told my brother I was going to send in my Chiller Blurb and tell you how much I love your books, but he says that you won't print it. Will you print my Chiller Blurb to prove my brother wrong? P.S: He loves your books just as much as I do."

-Garrett G., age 11, Arizona

"You came to our school last year and were really funny! Everyone in our school wants you to come back!"

-Maria F., age 8, Delaware

"I got five of your books for my birthday, and they were all autographed by you! Thank you so much! It was the best birthday gift EVER!"

-Paul D, age 10, North Dakota

"I can't wait to read OGRES OF OHIO! That's where I live! My dad thinks the title is funny, and he says that he's the REAL Ogre of Ohio!"

-Erin T., age 11, Ohio

"You are my favorite author! I can't believe you've written so many books! Do you wear those creepy glasses when you write your books? Do they help you make your books even scarier?"

-Brad S., age 10, South Carolina

"I just found out that you're going to write a book for every state! How long is it going to take you to do that? Please hurry up, because I can't wait to read all of them!"

-Robyn W., age 13, Maine

Got something cool to say about Johnathan Rand's books? Let us know, and we might publish it right here! Send your short blurb to:

Chiller Blurbs
281 Cool Blurbs Ave.
Topinabee, MI 49791

AMERICA'S #1 SERIES FOR MAXIMUM CHILLS!

#36: Carnivorous Crickets of Colorado

Johnathan Rand

An AudioCraft Publishing, Inc. book

This book is a work of fiction. Names, places, characters and incidents are used fictitiously, or are products of the author's very active imagination.

Book storage and warehouses provided by Chillermania!©
Indian River, Michigan

No part of this publication may be reproduced in whole or in part, or stored in a retrieval system, or transmitted in any form or by any means, electronic, mechanic, photocopying, recording, or otherwise, without written permission from the publisher. For information regarding permission, write to: AudioCraft Publishing, Inc., PO Box 281, Topinabee Island, MI 49791

American Chillers #36: Carnivorous Crickets of Colorado
ISBN 13-digit: 978-1-893699-68-7

Librarians/Media Specialists:
PCIP/MARC records available **free of charge** at
www.americanchillers.com

Cover illustration by Dwayne Harris
Cover layout and design by Sue Harring

Printed in USA

Carnivorous
Crickets
of
Colorado

VISIT CHILLERMANIA!

WORLD HEADQUARTERS FOR BOOKS BY JOHNATHAN RAND!

Visit the HOME for books by Johnathan Rand! Featuring books, hats, shirts, bookmarks and other cool stuff not available anywhere else in the world! Plus, watch the American Chillers website for news of special events and signings at **CHILLERMANIA!** with author Johnathan Rand! Located in northern lower Michigan, on I-75! Take exit 313 . . . then south 1 mile! For more info, call (231) 238-0338. And be afraid! Be veeeery afraaaaaaiiiid . . . .

1

When most people think of the word 'carnivore,' they tend to think of vicious, meat-eating creatures, such as dinosaurs or tigers. Or sharks, killer whales, polar bears . . . any number of animals around the world that prefer eating meat over plants. After all, that's what the word carnivore means: any animal that eats meat.

But *crickets?*

No one—including myself—would ever think of tiny crickets as dangerous predators. Crickets are just harmless, little insects that make soothing, chirping sounds by rubbing their wings together. Some crickets chirp during the day, some chirp all night long. They eat vegetation, not meat.

And there are different kinds of crickets: camel crickets, bush crickets, ant crickets, spider crickets, sand crickets, and more. In some countries, crickets are considered a delicacy, and people actually *eat* them! That just seems *so* gross. You would never catch me eating an insect in a million years. I don't care if I was starving. Just the thought of putting a bug in my mouth and chewing it up makes me want to puke. Yuck.

Most people in America are familiar with common field crickets that are found just about everywhere. These are small, shiny, black crickets that usually get no bigger than an inch. They're harmless. Field crickets are tiny and innocent and have never posed a threat to human beings. There has never been a good reason to be afraid of average, ordinary field crickets . . . until one horrifying day last summer in Aspen, Colorado.

But it had nothing to do with harmless, little crickets. No, the madness that began that horrible day wasn't because of small, chirping insects. It was caused by gigantic, predatory monsters—enormous field crickets of huge proportions—all brought about by an experiment that went horribly, horribly wrong.

2

My name is Kendra Delaney, and I live in Aspen, Colorado. Although I've lived here all of my life and I've been to only a few other states, I can tell you that Aspen is probably one of the prettiest places in the United States. Sure, there are many other great places in the country. But Aspen has everything that I love: mountains, forests, rivers, streams, and lakes. The people are very friendly and nice.

But best of all, Aspen has snow. Tons and tons and tons of snow. Not all year, of course.

However, during the winter, it's common to get several feet of snow and even more farther up in the mountains.

Which is one of the reasons why Aspen is one of the most popular skiing destinations . . . not only in the country, but in the world. People come from all over to ski the fresh, powdery snow and take in the beautiful, majestic surroundings of Aspen.

I'm a great skier and snowboarder. My dad taught me how to do both when I was very little, so skiing and snowboarding are as natural to me as walking or running. Winter, as you can imagine, is my very favorite time of year. Oh, there's nothing wrong with summertime. I like the warm weather, hiking in the woods, and swimming in the pool, lakes, and rivers.

It's just that I love winter so very, very much. All summer long, I look forward to our first snowfall. I look forward to the ski resorts opening up. I look forward to wearing my cold-weather gear and hanging out with my friends on the slopes.

But there is another reason altogether why I like winter better than summer. Winter is the time when the animals hibernate, the time for insects to go away. But spring always follows winter, and summer follows spring . . . which means the return of mosquitoes, bees, grasshoppers, houseflies, and all sorts of other insects.

Including crickets.

I know it sounds silly, but just the sound of that word—*crickets*—makes my blood turn cold and my skin turn to ice. I imagine you would feel the same way, too, if what happened to me happened to you.

Looking back, I should have known that something was wrong in July of last year. Two of my friends—Kiersten Cooper and Bryson Hatfield—and I had been hiking in the woods on a trail near our house. The trail winds through a thick forest, but there are also sections of rock that jut up into the air like canyon walls. The path passes by an old abandoned farm with several barns and a large pasture. Never before had we seen anyone in or around the old farm.

Until one day last July.

Bryson was the first to see something unusual, and he stopped walking. I was right behind him, followed by Kiersten, and the two of us stopped, too.

"Look at that," Bryson said.

Kiersten and I stepped around Bryson to have a look. In the driveway of the old abandoned farm was a big box truck about half the size of a semi-trailer. It sort of resembled a giant, square bug, with a white cab for its head and a white block for its body. On the side of the box was a cartoon character of a large, black cricket. Above the insect were the words

Carpenter's Cricket Farm
Crickets for Any Purpose

"What does that mean?" Kiersten asked. "I

mean . . . what do you use crickets for?"

Bryson shrugged. "My dad uses them for fishing bait," he said. "He usually buys them at the sporting goods store. I guess I never thought about where crickets came from."

"That's it, then," I said. "They're probably going to raise crickets and sell them to sporting goods stores, so they can sell them to fishermen."

At the time, it seemed a little strange that someone would try to raise crickets in Aspen, Colorado. I guess I just figured that the cold weather would kill the crickets in the winter, and I thought that there might be other places in the country that would be better to raise insects, somewhere warmer, like maybe Arizona or California. Or maybe some of the southern states like Mississippi, Alabama, or Georgia.

While we watched, a man walked to the back of the truck. He raised a large door that rolled up, and what we saw made our jaws drop.

Inside the truck were two *gigantic* crickets, nearly as tall as the man himself!

3

The three of us were spellbound, horrified, and mystified.

"*Holy cow,*" Bryson breathed. *"Look at those things."*

However, after a moment, we realized what we were seeing. The crickets weren't alive; they were simply large replicas of insects. While we watched, the man called to yet another man who came to his assistance. Together, they pulled out a ramp stowed away beneath the truck and carefully carried the two monstrous insects out of the white box, placing the motionless, giant bugs in the grass. Now that they were out of the truck and in the open, we could see that the characteristics of the insects were over exaggerated and cartoon-like.

"They must be using them as advertisements," Kiersten said.

"I'd like to have one of those in my front yard," Bryson said. "Could you imagine what people would think when they drove by? At a glance, those things look real."

I laughed. "Yeah," I said. "That would be pretty funny, all right."

Just then, one of the men turned and looked in our direction. I waved, and the man waved back.

"Let's go and say hi," I said, and the three of us began walking again.

When we arrived at the truck, the two men were leaning against it, resting. Nearby, the two gigantic cricket statues glistened in the sun.

"Hi," I said, waving my hand.

"Hello," one of the men said. He was wearing blue jeans, a red T-shirt, and a white baseball cap.

"Are you moving in?" Bryson asked.

The man with the baseball cap nodded. "That's right," he said. "Still have a lot of work to do to get the place ready, though."

Kiersten pointed at the two enormous cricket statues. "Are you guys opening a cricket farm?"

The other man was wearing brown overalls with a white T-shirt. He had thick, long, dark brown hair pulled into a ponytail.

"Right again," he said. "I'm Bill Carpenter, and this is my brother, Brad."

Brad, wearing a baseball cap, nodded.

"Are you raising crickets so you can sell them?" I asked. I know it seemed like a silly question, but I was still a bit mystified as to why someone would have a cricket farm in Colorado.

Bill Carpenter nodded. "We've been raising crickets our entire life," he said. "We sell them to sporting goods stores and pet stores."

Bryson frowned. "Pet stores?" he said. "People have crickets for pets?"

Bill and Brad Carpenter erupted into laughter.

"No, no," Brad said, shaking his head. "We sell them to pet stores, and they sell them to people who feed the crickets to their pets."

Again, Bryson frowned. "You mean dogs and cats eat crickets?"

Once again, Bill and Brad broke into a fit of laughter.

"Of course not," Bill said. "But lots of people have exotic pets like lizards, iguanas, snakes, and tarantulas. They need to eat, just like any other pet."

I guess I'd never thought of that. But, then again, I've never had a pet like that. We have a cat named Spaceman, and all we feed him, of course, is cat food.

Kiersten pointed to an address and a telephone number on the side of the truck. "Is that where you're from?" she asked. "Louisiana?"

Bill and Brad nodded. "We still have an operation in Baton Rouge," Brad answered. "But we want to try an experiment, and we need a location that has colder temperatures for five or six months out of the year."

"And Aspen seemed like the perfect place," Bill continued. "The summers here are warm, and the winters are cold with lots of snow. That's what we need for our experiment."

I was just about to ask another question, but Kiersten beat me to it.

"What kind of experiment?" she asked.

Bill and Brad looked at each other. They seemed reluctant to speak. Finally, Brad replied.

"Well," he said, "we just can't say right now. Cricket farming is a competitive business, and we don't want any of our competitors to find out what we're up to. If our experiment works, we'll have the biggest cricket farming operation in the country, and quite possibly the entire world."

"We'll be famous," Bill said, with a proud nod.

While we had no idea what their experiment was all about, we would soon learn one thing for sure: it was going to backfire in the worst way imaginable . . . and it wouldn't be long before Kiersten, Bryson, and I were in a battle with giant insects, fighting for our lives.

4

Fall came, followed by winter, and it was one of the best seasons ever. It snowed and snowed and snowed from October through April. There was always fresh snow on the slopes and in the woods. On top of that, we had a number of snow days, and school was canceled. On those days, Bryson, Kiersten, and I went snowboarding and skiing.

And by the time the snow melted in the spring, by the time the days were getting warmer, and I began to notice a few flowers blooming and insects buzzing around, I'd forgotten all about the

Carpenter brothers and their cricket farming operation in the old farmhouse in the woods . . . until one day in June when I noticed something very strange in the woods not far from our house.

I had called Bryson and Kiersten to see if they wanted to go to a nearby park, but Bryson had a dentist appointment, and Kiersten was busy helping her mom with something. It was a nice day, so I decided to go for a walk in the woods. I took our cat, Spaceman. We adopted Spaceman a couple of years ago. Actually, it was Spaceman who adopted us. He showed up on our doorstep one day, skinny and scraggly. We took him in, and to my surprise, Mom and Dad really liked him. It was Dad's idea to call him Spaceman, because he was all black with white around his face. He looked like he was wearing a white space helmet.

The funny thing is that Spaceman thinks he's a dog. He follows me around everywhere, especially when we're outside. Although we keep him in our house, he likes to go on walks with me.

He walks right behind me and never runs away. He doesn't seem the least bit interested in catching mice or birds, either. And at night, he curls up and sleeps at the foot of my bed. He loves attention and affection, and he loves it when I scratch him behind his ears and rub his back.

On this particular day, I set out on the trail that winds through the woods behind our house. Spaceman was right behind me. The day was sunny and warm. Birds chirped in the trees, and once in a while a mosquito buzzed by my head.

I continued walking along the trail until I saw the old farmhouse in the distance. I had forgotten all about the Carpenter brothers and their cricket farm, but now I wondered how they were doing and whether their experiment, whatever it was, had worked. Probably not, because I hadn't heard or seen anything about them on television or in the newspapers. If their experiment had worked, they thought they would be famous. Apparently, that wasn't the case.

Suddenly, I was struck with the feeling that

I was being watched, and I stopped on the trail. I slowly turned my head, peering through the woods, around branches and tree limbs. Spaceman rubbed against my leg, arching his back and purring. He didn't seem to sense that anything or anyone was watching us.

Still, I had an odd feeling, and I couldn't shake it.

I looked at the old farmhouse in the distance. It was too far away to really see much of anything, except a large barn and part of the house. There didn't seem to be anyone around.

Brushing off my uneasiness, I took a step forward . . . and that's when something exploded from its hiding place in the bushes and came right at me.

5

The movement was so sudden, so fast, that I didn't even have a chance to move. A large, dark creature bounded out from the brush and landed on the trail a few feet in front of me.

At first I thought it was a dog, but it was moving so fast that I didn't instantly recognize it. In the next moment, I realized it was a raccoon. He had probably been sleeping near the trail, and I had surprised him.

In two seconds, he was gone, crashing through the forest. Then, the only thing I heard were chirping birds and the thrashing of my heart in my chest.

I laughed out loud. "Wow, Spaceman," I said, with a chuckle. "That raccoon really freaked me out."

I looked down. Spaceman was no longer at my feet.

"Spaceman?" I said, looking around. "Where are you, buddy?"

Spaceman's head appeared from behind a tree farther back along the trail. He had been freaked out, too, and had fled to hide.

"It's okay," I said. "It was only a raccoon." I know it sounds silly to talk to my cat like he can actually understand me, but I do it all the time. Spaceman is as much of a friend to me as anyone. And besides: sometimes, I think he really *can* understand me.

Spaceman scampered back onto the trail and ran up to me. I began walking again, shaking my head and smiling. The raccoon had really given me a start.

"It's a good thing it wasn't a bear, Spaceman," I said. We have black bears in Colorado, and it's not uncommon to see them, especially farther up in the mountains. But sometimes, they can be a nuisance. One time, a black bear destroyed our bird feeder to get at the sweet seeds it contained. Occasionally, bears will tip over garbage cans in search of food. Some black bears have even been known to attack humans, which is a scary thought.

However, bears don't like humans all that much, and if you make noise while hiking in the woods, most bears will hear it and keep away. But if you are too quiet and sneak up on a bear, well, that could be a recipe for big trouble.

Mindful of this, I began whistling a tune as I walked, heading toward the old farmhouse. I didn't know this at the time, of course, but while I walked and whistled with Spaceman at my heels, several pairs of strange, sinister eyes were watching, hidden in the depths of the dark shadows of the forest. Bizarre, man-eating creatures—vicious carnivores—that I never knew existed were waiting for just the right moment to make their move . . . .

6

I should have known something was wrong the moment that Spaceman made a sudden leap from the trail into my arms. It was unexpected, but I managed to catch him and hold him to my chest.

I stopped walking.

"What's up with you, Spaceman?" I asked as I scratched my cat behind his ears. Usually when I do this, he closes his eyes and purrs. Now, however, his eyes were wide, dark marbles with golden diamonds nervously twitching back and forth, glancing around the forest.

"What's wrong, buddy?" I asked. "Is there another raccoon around?"

I tried to spot a raccoon that might be laying on the ground nearby or perhaps sitting on a tree branch not far away, looking at us. Raccoons can blend in so well that it's almost impossible to see them if they don't move.

But I didn't see a raccoon, or any other animal, for that matter. The only things I saw were a few birds flitting among the branches, chirping and singing.

Carrying Spaceman, I continued walking, scratching his ears and rubbing the back of his neck.

"Don't worry," I said. "I'm here to protect you. No evil raccoon is going to hurt you."

As I drew closer and closer to the old farmhouse, I began to feel something wasn't right. It wasn't a feeling that someone was watching me, it was just a feeling that something was wrong, but I couldn't put my finger on it. I didn't feel frightened, but I knew something wasn't as it should be.

Once again, I stopped walking. I continued to stroke Spaceman's neck, and he continued to gaze nervously into the forest around us. I've never seen him act like this before, and it was starting to make me nervous, too.

A large, chain-link fence bordered the trail and surrounded the pasture behind the farmhouse. It hadn't been there before, and I figured that the Carpenter brothers had probably built it. However, at the top of the fence, barbed wire was coiled and looped around the entire radius of the fence.

If they're only raising crickets, I wondered, *why on Earth would they need a fence topped with barbed wire?*

That just didn't make sense.

But, then again, maybe the chain-link fence and the barbed wire were put there to keep other creatures from getting inside. I wondered what kind of animal in Aspen would be so interested in crickets, but I couldn't come up with anything. Snakes would probably be interested in crickets, for sure. But snakes could easily slip through the fence, so I was sure it wasn't built to keep them out.

"It just doesn't make sense," I said to Spaceman.

I walked up to the fence. The ground on the other side had been torn up, like someone had taken a backhoe to it. No grass grew. The entire pasture was nothing but broken clumps of earth.

And, oddly enough, the entire farm, including the house and barns, looked abandoned, like no one had been there for a long time. I didn't see any sign of Bill or Brad Carpenter, and I didn't see their truck.

But I *did* see something that immediately sparked my interest.

I hadn't noticed it before, but not far from where I stood, a gigantic hole had been torn through the fence. The sharp points of the broken chain-links extended outward, as if something from inside had broken out.

Obviously, the Carpenter brothers were

raising more than just crickets. After all: crickets were just harmless, little insects, and the hole in the fence looked like it had been created by something much larger, something strong enough to rip a hole in a chain-link fence.

What kind of animal can do that? I wondered.

Suddenly, Spaceman stiffened in my arms. He was staring into the forest as he began hissing, his body rigid as I held him to my chest.

I peered into the forest, but saw nothing.

And that's when the eerie chirping began . . . .

7

The sound came from deep in the forest, and there was no mistaking what it was: crickets. I've heard enough crickets during my lifetime to know the sound they make. I know that during the day, crickets will make a different sound than at night.

What was most unusual about the sound was that it seemed to be coming from far, far away. It was the same tone and pitch of any other ordinary cricket, but the sound seemed to echo through the forest, growing louder and louder, filling my ears. At first, it was just a single cricket.

Soon, the sound was joined by yet another loud, booming chirping that came from another direction entirely.

Then, another joined in.

And another.

They all seemed to be quite a ways away, but the chirping sounded thick and full, like high-pitched jet engines.

Spaceman was terrified, and I held him tightly. His head snapped around, back and forth, searching the forest. His actions made me nervous, and I, too, looked around to see if there was anything in the woods.

Then, the chirping stopped all at once, as if an invisible signal had been given. I noticed that all other sounds had vanished, too. Birds were no longer singing in the trees. There was no wind, and the trees were frozen in silence, still and unmoving.

The silence was eerie. I have never been in the forest when things were so quiet. There were always things to hear: birds singing, insects buzzing, a breeze slithering through branches and leaves.

Now, the silence was overwhelming, and I know the comparison may seem odd, but the quiet seemed deafening. There was a roar in my ears that was nothing but silence.

Spaceman was trembling in my arms. The poor little guy was terrified. As for me, I was more mystified and curious than anything. The silence was unnerving, and I slowly turned around, peering expectantly into the heavy, deep shadows of the forest, searching for anything, looking for movement. When I had made a complete circle, I stopped.

Poor Spaceman was still trembling in my arms. I placed him on the ground, but he remained at my feet, trembling against my leg, looking around nervously.

The sound I heard next began with a snapping of branches and then a heavy crash, like a tree falling. This was followed by another crash, and another.

I turned in the direction of the noise. Spaceman scratched frantically at my pant leg, and I picked him up once again. All the while, I stared into the forest in the direction of the crashing sounds.

Still, I saw nothing, but there was no mistaking it. There was something coming my way.

Something *big*.

8

I stood frozen on the trail, listening, clutching Spaceman to my chest. The crashing sounds continued, closer and closer.

Then, in the distance, I saw a treetop move, as if the entire tree was being savagely pushed aside.

What can possibly be so big that it can push trees out of its way? I thought.

Regardless of what it was, I wasn't going to stand around and wait. Anything that big was bound to be a danger. Besides: Spaceman had a good instinct about these things. He was terrified. And if Spaceman was that afraid, it was all the more reason to worry. I needed to get away, and fast.

I was becoming frantic. I could run home, which would probably be the safest thing to do. Or I could run to the old farmhouse and probably find some place to hide, a place where I could remain out of sight and get a look at whatever creature or animal was coming.

I was torn between the two decisions. While I really wanted to be safe, I also wanted to know what was making the enormous crashing sounds. I couldn't imagine anything that big; no animal that I knew of that lived in Colorado could be making such a loud crashing sound. It truly sounded like an elephant or a rhinoceros was making its way through the forest.

Without thinking anything more about it, I began running down the trail toward the old farmhouse and the barns. Although the farmhouse looked abandoned, perhaps Bill or Brad Carpenter were home. Maybe it only appeared abandoned because I didn't see anyone or any vehicles in the driveway.

There were three large outbuildings, barns of different sizes, situated not far from the house. They were white, with big double doors in the front. All of the doors were closed, except for one.

That was just what I needed. I could slip inside the barn where Spaceman and I could remain hidden and possibly get a glimpse of the animal that was thundering through the forest.

"It's okay, buddy," I said to Spaceman. "We're going to be okay."

I paused for a moment to turn and look into the forest. I could still see branches and treetops being pushed and knocked over by the weight of some crushing animal, but I couldn't see what it was.

And I'm not sure that I really wanted to.

Clutching Spaceman to my chest with both arms, I ran the short distance to the barn. I paused briefly to look around, hoping to see Bill or Brad

Carpenter, but there was no sign of them. No sign of their vehicle, nothing that would indicate that anyone had even been at the farmhouse recently.

Strange.

The loud crashing and snapping of trees in the forest was closer than ever, and I wasted no time as I darted through the open barn door . . . where I found myself face-to-face with a huge insect, leering at me from the dark shadows!

9

It was with overwhelming relief that I quickly discovered that the giant cricket staring me down from the shadows wasn't alive; it was one of the fake insects that we'd spotted last year, when the Carpenter brothers were moving their operation to the farmhouse. In the shadows of the dimly-lit barn, however, the creature looked very real and lifelike. Farther back in the barn, I could pick out the silhouette of the other cricket leaning against the wall.

I stepped farther into the barn, away from

the door, immersing myself in the shadows. Outside, I could still hear the loud crashing sounds getting closer and closer. It really *did* sound like trees were falling, and I shuddered to think what kind of creature could be causing such destruction. I knew that there were specially-designed fire trucks made to go deep into the wilderness. These vehicles had enormous tires and reinforced frames and bumpers. They were specifically made to knock over trees so firefighters could travel deep into the woods to fight forest fires.

But they were loud, and their engines were deafening. Whatever was creating the sound that I was now hearing wasn't a machine, as I heard no motor. The only things I could hear were the heavy crackling and crunching of large branches and trunks as they snapped and limbs snapping as they hit one another.

Spaceman squirmed in my arms. He wasn't trembling as badly now, but I knew that he was still terrified. He stared curiously out the barn door, yet just as scared as ever.

Slowly, I retreated into the shadows. I knew it would be only a matter of moments before I would see something. I knew that whatever was creating the thundering, crashing sounds was about to emerge from the forest and cross the trail that I had been on. It would be only a few moments before I would see what it was, and I wanted to remain hidden from view. It would be best to stay unseen, especially because I didn't know what I was dealing with.

Again, I wondered what could possibly be in the forest.

Runaway elephant? Prehistoric woolly mammoth? A giant alien from outer space? I know that my thoughts were just plain silly and ridiculous, but my mind just couldn't fathom what could possibly be crashing through the forest, knocking down trees, snapping thick tree trunks and branches like they were toothpicks.

But when the gargantuan creature finally appeared and stopped on the trail, I knew that my wildest imagination could have never dreamed up what I was now looking at.

On the trail near the fence stood a single, blue cricket that was normal in every way except one:

He was over twenty feet tall!

10

I felt Spaceman stiffen in my arms. He began to hiss, but I gently covered his mouth and backed even farther into the darkness of the barn.

"Shhh," I whispered, tightly clutching Spaceman to my chest. He stopped hissing, but his body was still tight and tense. Both of us could only stare in amazement at the giant, blue insect that had appeared from the forest.

Never in my life had I been so afraid. But, then again, never in my life had I ever been confronted with such an impossible sight. I blinked several times, wondering if the creature was simply part of my imagination. When it didn't go away, I realized that what I was seeing was real. Although I wished that what I was seeing wasn't there, I knew that wishing wasn't going to do any good. Spaceman was seeing the same thing that I was, as he was absolutely terrified.

The giant, blue cricket just stood in the middle of the trail, not doing anything, except slowly waving his antennae back and forth. His blue body shined in the sun. I remembered learning in school that many insects have what is called an exoskeleton, meaning that their shell-like skeleton is on the outside of their bodies, which serves to protect their insides. Humans, in contrast, have an endoskeleton located within their bodies, beneath the flesh.

Thoughts pinwheeled through my brain. *Where did he come from? How was it possible?*

I was certain that the giant, blue cricket had something to do with the experiments that the Carpenter brothers had talked about.

What kind of experiments have been conducted? I thought. *Was this their plan all along? To create enormous crickets the size of elephants?*

And if so: *why?* Of what use could these creatures possibly be? They were too big to fish with, and you certainly weren't going to feed a twenty-foot cricket to a pet iguana!

These thoughts did nothing to stifle the horror that had gripped my entire body, although I was comforted by the fact that I was in the barn, and I was sure that the insect hadn't spotted me. However, for the time being, I wasn't about to move. Something told me that if I tried to make a run for it, I would be overtaken by that monstrous thing within seconds.

So, at least for the moment, it was going to be a waiting game. I wasn't going anywhere until I knew that giant insect was far, far away.

The blue cricket stopped waving his two antennae. He was completely motionless.

Then:

Another sound. More crashing in the forest,

followed by a moment of silence.

Suddenly, a movement in the sky caught my attention. In the next instant, another enormous cricket, this one shiny black, landed with a thunderous crash inside the fenced-in pasture. The ground shook as the enormous insect crashed to Earth.

In my arms, Spaceman trembled, then hissed.

"Shhh, buddy," I whispered. *"Shhh."*

The shiny, black cricket in the fenced-in pasture was nearly as big as the enormous, blue cricket on the trail. His body glistened like shiny, black armor in the late morning sun.

Just how many of these things are there in the forest? I wondered. It was a frightening thought. If there were two, there were probably more. It was obvious that whatever experiments the Carpenter brothers had conducted, they'd gone horribly, horribly wrong.

Then again, maybe not. Maybe this was exactly what they intended. Maybe they had wanted to create gigantic creatures, monstrous insects of gargantuan proportions.

I heard another noise and flinched. This time, the noise wasn't from the outside of the barn, nor was it nearly as loud as the crashing through the forest. It came from a few feet away, in the shadows of the barn.

Slowly, I turned my head and looked down . . . horrified to see two, large gleaming eyes staring back at me from the darkness . . . .

11

I held my breath. While I wasn't sure exactly what I was looking at, I had my suspicions. Whatever it was, it was too big to be a mouse or a rat, too big to be a cat or a dog. It was some sort of live creature, for sure, because while I watched, it moved to the side, closer to the barn wall, and I wondered if it had spotted me. Perhaps not.

So, I remained completely motionless, staring at whatever was glaring back at me from the murky shadows.

Spaceman had spotted the creature, too, and

he shuddered in my arms.

Outside of the barn, the giant, black cricket made a sudden leap over the fence, high into the air, where he came crashing down on top of the blue cricket! The two enormous insects battled, wrestling and rolling, knocking over trees and saplings as they grappled with one another. They gave off strange chirping noises, high-pitched grunts and squeals that echoed through the forest.

Then, I remembered another story I heard recently about giant mosquitoes in Maine. Apparently, the mosquitoes had some sort of reaction when they bit some horses that had been treated with a special medication. This had caused the mosquitoes to grow to enormous sizes. In fact, a couple of innocent kids barely escaped with their lives.

But at least there was an explanation for the giant mosquitoes. Right now, there was no explaining the truly monstrous crickets that were now battling before me.

I began to wonder if Spaceman and I were

safe, after all. If those crickets rolled toward us, they would easily crush the barn. We would be squished like bugs.

A human and her cat squished by bugs, I thought. For a moment, it was almost funny.

But that moment vanished quickly. I was in big, big trouble, and I knew it. So was Spaceman.

The giant insects rolled farther to the right, and I could no longer see them. I could certainly hear them, though, as they battled one another. I wondered if it was a fight to the death. Would the blue cricket kill the black one? Or would the black one kill the blue one?

Most important, I was thinking about a way to escape. With the crickets focused on fighting each other, maybe I would have an opportunity to get away.

I slowly turned my head and looked at the beady eyes that were still glaring at me from the shadows. While I watched, the creature began to move. It crawled forward, then began inching toward the door.

Two things were immediately apparent. First of all, it *was* a cricket, there was no doubt about it. It was much, much smaller than the ones doing battle outside of the barn, but it was still enormously big. The insect was about the size of a full-grown German Shepherd, but it was yellow in color, like a faded lemon.

And even more important, either the cricket didn't see me, or it wasn't paying attention. It was only a few feet away from Spaceman and me, but the thing just ignored us. It crawled toward the open barn door, then stopped. The insect seemed interested in watching the other two crickets do battle. Spaceman trembled in my arms, and I tried to hold him tightly to comfort him, but I think I was shaking just as badly!

Then, with a sudden leap, the cricket launched into the air and landed about twenty feet away, on the other side of the chain-link fence.

A lump formed in my throat, and I swallowed hard. I could still hear the other two crickets fighting, but I couldn't see them.

Should I try to make a run for it? If I did, where would I go? If I tried to take the path home, I would run right in front of the battling crickets. They might decide to come after me, instead of fighting one another.

Cautiously, I took a few steps forward until I was in the doorway of the barn. The blue and black crickets continued to battle one another, but they had rolled to the other side of another barn, and I couldn't see them. Meanwhile, inside the fence, in the pasture, the yellow cricket looked on. He, too, was intensely interested in the battling crickets.

But from where I was, I had a straight shot to the old farmhouse. In two dozen steps, I could be at the front door.

The problem was, I was pretty sure that the door would be locked. It was obvious that the Carpenter brothers had abandoned their cricket farm and moved on to who knew where. I was sure that the windows were locked, too.

No, running to the house wasn't going to

work. There was no way I would be able to get inside.

Slowly, I left the barn and looked the other way, down the driveway.

Not a cricket in sight.

I had been down the driveway many times, before the Carpenter brothers bought the property. The driveway was long and bumpy, made of hard-packed dirt and gravel. It came out at a paved road about a half-mile from my house.

That seemed to be my best option. Behind me, on the other side of the barn, and in the pasture, were three freaks of nature: one yellow, one blue, and one black. I wanted to get as far away from them as I could, as quickly as possible.

"Are you ready for this, Spaceman?" I whispered.

I glanced at the yellow cricket in the confines of the pasture to make sure he wasn't watching us. Then, slowly and carefully, I lowered Spaceman to the ground. He could run just as fast as I could, probably faster. If we both ran on our own, we would be able to cover more distance than if I had to carry him in my arms. I was worried that we might run into other crickets during our escape, but that was a chance I would have to take.

I was just about ready to take off running when I heard another noise altogether, and turned.

Laughter.

It was distant, and I couldn't make out where it was coming from, but it was definitely the sound of kids laughing.

I looked down the trail that I had taken, the one that led from our house, through the woods into the old farmhouse. I didn't see anything . . . at first.

Then, a shape came into view. Someone on a bicycle.

All too late, I realized who it was.

Bryson.

Not only that, but Kiersten was right behind him. Both were on their bicycles, and both were completely unaware of the enormous crickets battling in the yard near the old farmhouse. They had no idea there was a giant yellow cricket in the pasture, waiting and watching.

What are they doing here? I wondered. *Bryson had a dentist appointment, and Kiersten was supposed to be helping her mother.*

I opened my mouth to shout a warning, but it was too late. The yellow cricket, already hearing the laughter, was ready. He crouched down and sprang dozens of feet into the air, easily clearing the fence. With yet another powerful bound, he sprang into the air again, over the treetops, and landed on the trail . . . right in front of Bryson and Kiersten!

12

The giant, yellow cricket blocked my view of Bryson and Kiersten, so I wasn't able to see their reaction when the monstrous insect suddenly landed in front of them. But their screams of horror told me everything I needed to know.

While I watched, the yellow cricket lunged forward, in full attack mode. Kiersten suddenly appeared to the left of the creature and darted into the forest. Bryson tumbled to the right, and after leaping to his feet, he, too, fled into the forest.

Without even thinking, I began running

toward them, toward the enormous, yellow cricket in the middle of the trail. I didn't know what I could do or what I would do, but I had to help my friends. After all: I was the reason they were here in the first place. I had told them that I would be on the trail.

After only a few dozen steps, I passed the barn that had prevented me from seeing the blue and black crickets that were fighting each other. Now they were in full view, and I could see them locked together, a mass of shiny, long arms and legs, still struggling in battle. They towered above me, and I felt very, very small and helpless.

Thankfully, they didn't pay any attention to me. I continued running down the trail toward the giant cricket that had attacked my friends. I could still hear both of them screaming in terror as they crashed into the woods. The yellow cricket, however, didn't make any attempt to chase after them. He just remained where he was, in the middle of the trail, facing the opposite direction.

I slowed to a walk, then stopped and turned

my head.

Behind me, the black and blue crickets continued fighting. They still hadn't seen me, or if they had, they weren't paying any attention.

I didn't see Spaceman, and I was glad. I was sure he'd find a place to hide, and he'd find me when the danger had passed.

I turned back around. I could see Kiersten's and Bryson's bicycles laying down on the trail.

But now, the giant, yellow cricket was facing me.

His two antennae waved back and forth like thin, wisping snakes.

His head shifted to the left, and then to the right.

His two antennae stopped moving.

Then, the creature crouched low. Before I could do anything about it, before I could even try to turn and flee, the cricket had lunged into the air. He landed directly on top of me, knocking me onto my back and pinning me to the ground!

13

The sudden attack knocked the wind from my lungs, and it was nearly impossible to breathe. On top of that, the giant, yellow cricket pinned me to the ground with several of his powerful legs. I tried to struggle and break free while I gasped for air, but my efforts were useless. The giant cricket was just too strong.

I tried to scream, but I had no voice. The only sounds I was able to make were choking heaves as I gasped for air.

The terrible creature looming over me

opened his mouth. I was able to manage a faint scream, but it was cut short as the terrible insect lunged down with his powerful jaws. I tried to twist once again, but it was just no use. I closed my eyes and waited for the worst, waited for the powerful jaws of the insect to chomp into my body.

In the next instant, the creature had moved to the side and released me. I didn't know how or why, and I didn't care. All I knew was that I could move, and I wasn't going to waste any time.

I leapt to my feet in time to see Bryson. He was carrying a long stick, wielding it like a spear, pointing it at the giant, yellow cricket. I couldn't believe Bryson's bravery! He had known I was in trouble and had returned to help. He had probably poked at the cricket with the long branch, not knowing whether it would make any difference.

However, he had disturbed the cricket, and the giant insect had moved off of me and was now squaring off with Bryson.

"Run!" Bryson urged as he stood his ground. "Get away from him, Kendra!"

"You can't fight that thing with a stick!" I shouted back.

Kiersten suddenly emerged from the forest and appeared on the trail. She had a large rock in her hand, and she launched it at the cricket. It struck one of the insect's legs, and the creature turned to face his newest opponent.

Seeing my two friends and their acts of bravery gave me a surge of hope. Kiersten and Bryson had come to my aid, even though they knew their chances of succeeding against such a giant monstrosity weren't very good. But they had succeeded . . . at least for the time being.

Kneeling down, I reached out and grabbed a softball-sized rock. I stood and hurled the stone at the insect as hard as I could. It struck the giant creature on its back, then harmlessly bounced away and tumbled to the ground. It had little effect except to draw the insect's attention for a moment.

When the cricket turned toward me, Bryson seized the opportunity to lunge. He leapt forward and poked the cricket with his stick, which drew the attention of the insect once again.

Meanwhile, Kiersten had already picked up another rock. She threw it at the cricket's head. It was a direct hit, but it had no other effect except to momentarily draw the attention of the insect as the rock bounced off and fell to the ground.

Finally, in frustration, the insect crouched down, paused, then leapt high into the air and vanished over the treetops. We could hear him land in the forest as branches and trees snapped, but we couldn't see where he was.

Bryson and Kiersten saw the black and blue crickets still locked in battle near the barn. The insects had each other in death grips and appeared to have each other paralyzed. Both refused to let go or give in.

"What is going on?!?!" Kiersten shrieked. "Where did those things come from?!?!"

"Let's figure that out later," Bryson said. "We've got to get away from them before they kill us!"

Without saying another word, the three of us instinctively began to run down the trail. Kiersten and Bryson would have the advantage of their bicycles, so once they reached them, they would be able to go faster. Still, I'm a fast runner, and I was hopeful that the three of us would be able to get away without encountering any more gigantic crickets. We'd figure out where they'd come from later. Right now, the most important thing was to get somewhere safe.

We had nearly reached the two bicycles when a dark shadow fell over us. The three of us looked up at the same time, only to see the enormous, blue cricket coming down upon us!

14

Bryson, Kiersten, and I stopped just in time and retreated backward. With an enormous crash, the giant, blue cricket landed on the trail in front of us. While we backed away, we watched, spellbound, as the cricket reared up, took Bryson's bike in its front legs, and began to chew on it as if it were candy!

"Follow me!" I shouted. "One of the barn doors is open. We can hide in there!"

Bryson and Kiersten followed me as I ran along the trail. The chain-link fence was on my right, and on my left, not far away at all, the black cricket was crouching low, as if he was trying to hide.

A few seconds later, we reached the barn and bounded through the open door. Bryson was the last one in, and he pulled the door shut. Immediately, we were swallowed by darkness. The darkness made me feel more secure, like we couldn't be seen. Still, I knew that we were sitting ducks. Those crickets were so big, I had no doubt they could easily tear the barn apart to get at us, if that's what they wanted.

"Where did those things come from?" Bryson asked. Although I couldn't see him, I could tell by his voice that he was only a few feet away from me.

"I have no idea," I replied. "The first one I saw was that big blue one. Then, the black one came, and the two began fighting. I tried to run away, but that yellow one attacked me. If you guys hadn't shown up when you did, I would have been cricket food."

"But this is impossible!" Kiersten said. "Crickets can't grow that big!"

"Remember what the Carpenter brothers told us last year?" I said. "Remember they told us they were going to do some sort of experiment that was going to make them famous. Maybe this is it. Maybe they created these giant crickets."

"But where did the brothers go?" Bryson asked.

"I'll bet the crickets ate them," Kiersten said.

It was a chilling thought, but I had to admit: Kiersten was probably right. Those crickets were bloodthirsty. I had no doubt that if Bryson hadn't shown up at that very second with his stick to distract the yellow cricket that had threatened me, I wouldn't be here right now.

"But crickets aren't meat eaters," Bryson said. Now that my eyes were getting accustomed to the dark, I could make out his faint silhouette and the shadow of Kiersten standing next to him.

"Not true," I said. "Crickets will eat just about anything."

"How do you know?" Kiersten asked.

"After the Carpenter brothers told me that they were going to raise crickets," I said, "I did a little investigating to see what cricket farming was all about. I didn't find out all that much, but I learned that crickets are easy to keep and raise if you have the right environment and proper food and water. Mostly, crickets are omnivorous."

"What does that mean?" Bryson asked.

"It means they mostly eat decaying plants, fungus, things like that," I replied. "However, if crickets are hungry, they will eat the bodies of dead crickets."

"Eww, gross," Kiersten said.

"Yeah," Bryson agreed.

"But I also found out that crickets have incredibly powerful jaws," I continued. "Some of them have been known to bite humans."

"Those crickets out there could do more than just bite," Bryson said. "Those crickets out there could chomp us completely in half. They're big enough to be able to swallow us in one gulp, without chewing."

"Well," I said. "At least we're safe for the time being. As long as we—"

I cut my sentence short when I heard a loud, painful squeal. Instantly, I knew who it was. With everything going on, I had forgotten about him until that very moment, but his painful wail suddenly filled me with horror.

Spaceman.

He had run one way to hide, while I had run in the opposite direction. I had escaped . . . but the sounds of my poor cat screeching told me that my best friend hadn't been so lucky.

15

Without thinking, I raced to the door, threw it open, and burst into the sunshine. Spaceman howled as frantically as ever, and my head snapped back and forth, searching for him.

There.

On the porch of the old farmhouse, a cricket had cornered my cat. The insect was a creamy, eggshell color and was about as tall as a normal adult human.

"Hey!" I shouted as I raced toward the insect.

"Kendra!" Bryson shouted. "What are you doing?!?!"

I ignored him. I didn't know what I was going to do, but I wasn't going to let that six-foot bug get my cat.

"Hey!" I shouted again as if the cricket would be able to understand me. Regardless, the sound of my voice drew his attention away from Spaceman. As soon as the cricket looked in my direction, Spaceman darted out from the corner of the porch and vanished around the side of the house. While I didn't know where he ran off to, at least he was out of danger . . . for the time being.

The eggshell-colored cricket turned to face me. I stopped, frantically wondering what to do. The best thing seemed to be to run back to the barn, but then what? We couldn't stay there all day. We had no idea what the crickets were after, what they were capable of, where they came from, or where they were going . . . if they were going anywhere.

No, we needed to find someplace safer, at

least until we knew we would be able to get away safely and go home.

"Kendra!" Bryson shouted. "Get back here! That thing is going to get you!"

I turned and looked down the trail, my eyes following the fence line and the coil of barbed wire that ran along top of it. In the distance, I saw the enormous, blue cricket. With one leg, it was holding what was left of Bryson's mangled bicycle, peering curiously at it, as if wondering why it tasted so bad.

Then, I looked back at the old farmhouse and at another barn not far away.

At ground level, next to the wall of the barn, were two doors. However, they were built at an angle, as if they might open to a staircase that went down into the earth, beneath the barn. I had seen these before. In some places of the country, they're used as storm cellars, safe havens during times of bad weather or tornadoes. In other parts of the country, people built them to store fruits, vegetables, and meats, because it's cooler in the ground.

The doors were made of metal and appeared much newer than the barn. I figured that the Carpenter brothers must have built some sort of underground storage area beneath the barn.

Regardless, it seemed like it would be a much safer place to hide. If the doors opened up to some sort of storm cellar, I was certain that they would lock on the inside. Steel doors were much more likely to keep the crickets out than the old, wooden barn doors.

"Kendra!" Bryson shouted again.

I pointed at the storm cellar doors while turning to face Bryson. He and Kiersten were standing in the open barn door, waiting for me.

"Over there!" I said. "There's a storm cellar or something that goes into the ground beneath the barn. We'll be safer there."

Bryson and Kiersten looked to where I was pointing. Without giving it a second thought, they took off running toward me. I, too, began to run toward the doors that hopefully would lead to a safe haven for us, somewhere we could hide without being threatened, somewhere we could collect our thoughts and figure out what we were going to do next.

An enormous crashing sound caused me to turn my head. Behind us, the enormous, blue cricket towered above the barn we had been hiding in. With just a single sweep of one of its powerful legs, most of the barn had been demolished. If Bryson and Kiersten had stayed there for just another few seconds, it would have been all over for them.

But that meant we had another problem. The big, blue insect was now focused on us, and I knew there was little chance of us making it to the storm cellar doors before he attacked us . . . and, at that very moment, that's precisely what the horrifying insect did.

16

When Kiersten saw the enormous, blue cricket bearing over her, she screamed. It was a high-pitched wail that echoed through the forest. We heard another loud crash, and I knew that the giant, blue cricket was laying waste to the rest of the barn. He didn't want to destroy the structure as much as he wanted to get at us, that much I was certain.

It didn't take me long to reach the storm cellar doors. Thankfully, they weren't locked, and I had no trouble throwing them open. It was with great relief that I saw wooden stairs sinking into the ground, beneath the barn, leading to a cellar or basement of some sort. The walls were made of concrete, as was the ceiling. I didn't take the time to count, but there were probably about a dozen steps in all.

I turned to look behind me. Kiersten and Bryson were running as fast as they could. Behind them, the enormous, blue cricket had completely demolished the barn and was in pursuit of my two friends.

"Faster!" I shouted.

Bryson and Kiersten reached the storm cellar and bounded inside. Bryson nearly tripped going down the steps, but Kiersten grabbed his shoulder and kept him from falling.

As soon as they were on their way down the steps, I followed. Just in time, too. As I slammed the metal doors closed behind me, the enormous insect reached out with its two front legs. If I hadn't closed the doors at that exact moment, he would have snared me in his powerful claws.

Instead, they slammed into the metal doors, causing them to shake.

Darkness fell over us, just like it had when the barn doors closed at our previous hiding spot. I brushed the palms of my hands over the inside of the door, searching. As I suspected, there was a lock on the inside. It was a long bolt, and I quickly slid it to the left, securing the doors.

The insect lashed out again, hitting the metal doors with its legs, but the lock held. I slowly backed down the steps in the darkness, feeling along the wall with my fingers for a light switch. They were met with nothing but rough cement.

There has to be a light somewhere, I thought.

I had just finished that thought when bright white light bloomed. At the bottom of the steps, Bryson had found a light switch. It was only a single bulb that dangled from the ceiling, but it gave off enough light to see our present surroundings.

I was still near the top of the steps, close to

the door, but Kiersten and Bryson had reached the dirt floor below, where the room opened up. Because I was near the top of the stairs, I couldn't see what was in the room.

They were looking around with stunned looks on their faces. Kiersten's mouth hung open as she slowly turned her head.

"What is it?" I asked as I began to descend the steps. "What's down here?"

Kiersten shook her head. "Kendra," she said, "you're going to have to see this to believe it."

17

It was a laboratory . . . sort of.

The room wasn't very big, maybe twice the size of my bedroom. Tables were pushed against the walls, and there were metal cages stacked on and beneath them. Also on the tables were several glass aquariums that had dried leaves, sticks, and a few rocks inside. In one corner was a pile of old newspapers.

"This must be where they raised the crickets," Kiersten said.

"I don't understand," Bryson said. "Why would they raise them down here, in a cellar? It seems like they would have much more room in the barns."

I walked to one of the tables and picked up a metal cage. It was about the size of a shoe box, and the wires were very close together. Looking closer, I found several places where the wires were broken and small holes were formed, as if something had chewed its way out.

"Look at this," I said.

Bryson and Kiersten walked to my side.

"Look at this," I repeated as I held up the cage for them to see. "It looks like something chewed its way out of here."

"Not just something," Bryson said. "A cricket is my guess."

"But how could ordinary crickets chew their way through metal?" Kiersten asked.

"Think about it, Kiersten," I said. "Those giant things outside aren't just normal crickets. They're bloodthirsty killers. Whatever experiments the Carpenter brothers were doing, they succeeded in creating those giant things out there."

"This is like something from a science fiction movie," Bryson said. "Stuff like this only happens in movies."

"There has to be an explanation," I said.

"I'll bet the Carpenter brothers were eaten by their own creations," Kiersten said. "They probably had no idea that their experiment was going to get so far out of hand."

The ground trembled, and we could hear muffled crashing sounds above us. I could only imagine the damage that the blue cricket was doing.

Kiersten walked to a table on the other side of the room and picked up something.

"Guys!" she exclaimed excitedly. "Look at this!"

I put the case back on the table, and Bryson and I hurried to Kiersten's side.

"What is it?" Bryson asked.

Kiersten was holding a large, three ring binder. It was black and contained what appeared to be hundreds of pages. She had opened it up and was flipping through the volume.

"It's a logbook of some sort," Kiersten said. "It looks like a record of their experiments and their progress."

She placed it on the table, and we began turning the pages. We didn't need to read everything to figure out what the Carpenter brothers had done. And we didn't have to read everything to figure out something else: the three of us, and quite possibly the entire city of Aspen, were in a lot of trouble.

18

Although Bill and Brad Carpenter had kept a very detailed record of their experiments, we didn't have to read every word or sentence to know that something had gone horribly wrong.

What they had been trying to do was create a hybrid cricket, a kind that could survive colder temperatures without dying or going into hibernation. On top of that, they wanted to create crickets that were two or three times the normal size of regular crickets.

While they hadn't succeeded in creating

crickets that could survive in colder climates, they were very successful in creating very large insects. They were so successful, in fact, that their project soon got out of hand. The journal described how the crickets became very ferocious and displayed incredible strength, changing colors as they grew. Their breeding quickly got out of control, and when some of the crickets escaped, they fled into the woods. The journal described a horrifying incident where Brad woke up one morning to find a giant cricket eating a deer!

But there was one paragraph that I read that circled through my mind over and over.

The crickets seem to have become carnivorous, preferring flesh and blood over any other food. Additionally, it appears that the crickets continue to grow. The more they eat, the bigger they get.

I thought about that.

The crickets seem to have become carnivorous, preferring flesh and blood over any other food. Additionally, it appears that the crickets continue to grow. The more they eat, the bigger they get.

The ground above us shook once again.

"Look here," Bryson said, pointing to the very last page. "Here's the last entry. Bill or Brad wrote that they were driving back to their main headquarters in Louisiana to get some special insecticide in a last-ditch effort to stop the crickets. They wrote that they would be returning on July 16th."

"That's today!" Kiersten said. "They're supposed to come back today!"

"That means all we have to do is wait," I said, with a sigh of relief. "The Carpenter brothers are going to be returning today. All we have to do is wait for them to come back, and everything will be okay."

And in a strange twist of fate, right at that very moment, we heard something: a faint rumbling sound. It grew louder and louder, until it was obvious it was the arrival of a truck.

"They're here!" Bryson exclaimed. "The Carpenter brothers made it back!"

The three of us were about ready to race

across the room and up the stairs, but we were stopped by an enormous crash. It was the sound of twisting metal, of shattering glass and snapping steel.

Then, those sounds were followed by awful, horrible, painful screaming . . . and the three of us knew that it was the end of the line for Bill and Brad Carpenter.

We also knew something else: it was probably the end of the line for us.

19

When the screaming stopped, all other sounds ceased. The only thing that we could hear was our own heavy breathing.

The three of us stood at the bottom of the stairs, looking up at the closed metal doors above us.

What had happened up there? I wondered. Obviously, something horrible. I don't think Bill and Brad Carpenter were prepared to deal with the crickets. According to their journal, they would have been gone for over a week. The crickets would have had all that time to continue eating and growing.

"What are we going to do?" Kiersten whispered.

"We have to find out what happened," Bryson said. "Somehow, we have to let someone know what's going on."

"But maybe Bill and Brad are okay," I said. "Or maybe they're hurt and need help."

"Only one way to find out," Bryson said. He took a step up, and Kiersten and I followed him. At the top of the stairs, he quietly slid the bolt back and pushed the metal door open a crack.

Sunlight streamed in as he pressed his face to the door.

"What do you see?" I asked.

Bryson shook his head. "I can't see anything from here," he replied. "I'm going to have to open the door farther."

"Be careful," Kiersten said.

Cautiously, Bryson pushed the door open farther. More light streamed in.

"I still can't see anything," he said.

He pushed the door open farther. Now, his entire head was outside.

"Oh, my gosh!" he whispered. "Their truck is completely destroyed!"

"Do you see Bill or Brad anywhere?" I asked.

Bryson shook his head slightly. "No," he replied. "I don't see them anywhere."

"They were probably eaten by that cricket," Kiersten said.

It was a gruesome thought, but Kiersten was probably right. Two human beings wouldn't stand a chance against a twenty-foot insect.

But if the Carpenter brothers had been eaten, our only hope of being rescued was gone. I had hoped that when Bill and Brad returned, they would be able to save us. Now, if we were going to stay alive, it was going to be up to us.

"Wait a minute," Bryson said. "The front door to the old farmhouse is open. Wasn't it closed before?"

"Yes," I replied. "It looked like all the doors

and windows were shut tight."

"Well," Bryson continued, "the front door is open a few inches. Maybe Bill and Brad made it into the house. Maybe they're safe."

"Do you see where that cricket went?" Kiersten asked.

"He's nowhere in sight," Bryson replied, turning his head. "At least I can't—"

Bryson's sentence was cut short as he was yanked violently up into the air. The metal door he had been holding open was nearly ripped from its hinges, and the last thing we saw before Bryson vanished was an enormous, blue claw gripping his waist!

20

Without giving it another thought, I raced up the steps. I had no idea what I was going to do, as I knew I was powerless to stop the giant cricket. But I had to try to do *something*. After all, Bryson had come to my aid once already. He had taken on a cricket that was much larger than he was.

But one look at the creature towering above told me that there was nothing I could do. The blue insect had been lurking around the side of the barn, unknown to Bryson, who had been looking in the other direction, at the old farmhouse. The enormous insect snapped up Bryson as easily as a child picks up a small stick.

Now, as I looked up at the horrific scene, I was once again reminded of some sort of strange science fiction movie. Once, I saw an old movie poster with King Kong, the giant gorilla, holding a woman in his palm. What I was seeing was just like that: a gigantic beast threatening a tiny, harmless person.

Bryson wasn't giving up without a fight. He was kicking and screaming, struggling to free himself from the viselike grip of the cricket. The insect was peering curiously at him, as if he had caught some strange sort of bug, the way a boy might behave if he had found some strange insect beneath a log. It was almost funny, and had Bryson not been in such imminent danger, I probably would have laughed out loud.

Near the Carpenter's mangled truck was a pile of rocks. I ran to them, picked one up, turned, and hurled it at the gigantic insect. The rock bounced off the creature's chest and had no effect at all.

Kiersten joined me, and the two of us began throwing rocks at the insect. I know that it didn't seem like we were doing much, but there really wasn't anything else we could do. We had no other weapon, no gun or knife or anything else but the rocks that we found scattered on the ground.

All the while, Bryson screamed louder and louder. The insect, I was sure, was crushing him with that single, powerful claw, and if we didn't do something fast . . . .

Kiersten threw a rock, aiming it at the giant insect's head. The stone wasn't very big, probably the size of a baseball, but it struck the giant cricket directly in one of its eyes. The insect responded by letting out a horrible, deafening squeal. He released Bryson, who fell nearly ten feet to the ground. He landed on his feet, but quickly crumpled to the ground, motionless.

But now the insect was enraged. He had spotted Kiersten and me and had set his sights on us.

"Run!" I shouted, and Kiersten went one way while I took off in the other direction, each of us racing around opposite sides of the old farmhouse. I nearly tripped on a log, but I caught myself before I fell. Recovering, I continued running around the side of the house until I reached the back.

To my great surprise, the back door of the farmhouse flew open. There, standing in the doorway, was Brad Carpenter! He was alive! Not only that, but his brother, Bill, was right behind him!

"Inside! Quick!" Brad said as he reached out, grabbed my hand, and pulled me into the house.

"Kiersten is still out there!" I said.

Just then, Kiersten rounded the corner. The shadow of the insect fell over the backyard just as she reached the door and leapt inside. Brad slammed the door closed.

In the backyard, the giant, blue cricket appeared. He snapped a nearby tree in half as if it were a toothpick.

"We thought you were dead!" I said, glancing at Bill, then Brad.

"Yeah," Kiersten huffed. "We thought you guys were eaten by that evil bug!"

"And Bryson is still in the front yard!" I exclaimed.

The four of us hustled down the hallway, through a large living room, and to the big picture window that faced the driveway and the barns. Bryson remained in the driveway where he had fallen, curled on his side.

"We've got to help him!" I said. "He might be okay. We've got to get him inside before that cricket eats him!"

"I'll get him," Brad said. "You guys stay here."

After making sure that the giant, blue cricket was still in the backyard, Brad opened the front door. Double-checking once again to make sure there were no crickets nearby, he darted off the porch and bolted across the driveway, past the mangled remains of their big box truck that lay sideways in the driveway.

Bryson must've heard Brad's footsteps, because he raised his head and crawled to his knees. As Brad reached him, Bryson stood up.

"We thought you were dead!" Bryson said.

"Are you okay?" Brad asked.

"I'm fine," Bryson said as he quickly brushed himself off. "I was just pretending that I was dead, hoping that thing would leave me alone."

Which was pretty smart, when you come to think of it. I've heard of people who were attacked by bears or other wild animals, and they had done the same thing: they played dead, and the attacking predator left them alone. It had saved their lives.

"Come on!" Brad urged. "We've got to get back to the house!"

But that wasn't going to happen. Without any warning whatsoever, an enormous, green cricket fell from the sky and landed in the driveway. The house trembled, windows rattled, pictures on the wall shook, and the earth beneath us shuddered. The huge, green insect lunged forward, its front legs raised, poised to strike in an instant. In the driveway, Bryson and Brad weren't going to stand a chance.

21

The giant beast lunged at Bryson and Brad the moment it landed, and the only thing that saved them from certain death was pure, dumb luck. Bryson ran to the left, while Brad ran to the right, momentarily confusing the insect. When it lashed out to grab one of them, its leg was met with nothing but air.

Bryson and Brad raced to the storm cellar, where they slammed the doors closed and vanished inside. The enraged, green cricket began clawing at the closed metal doors, but it was unsuccessful at opening them.

"Can't you stop them?" I asked. "We read in your journal that you went back to Louisiana to get some sort of insecticide that would kill the crickets."

Bill nodded. "And we did," he said. "The problem is that it's in a five-gallon drum in the back of our truck. A huge, blue cricket attacked us when we arrived and mangled our vehicle. We barely made it into the farmhouse alive."

"Can we go and get it?" Kiersten asked.

The three of us looked at the giant, green cricket. By now, he had become bored with trying to get into the storm cellar and was crawling toward the demolished barn.

Bill shook his head. "My brother and I probably could," he said, "but the container is too heavy for you guys. We would have to get it into the farmhouse to make it ready."

"What do you mean by that?" I asked.

"The insecticide in the drum is a concentrated powder," Bill explained. "It needs to be mixed with white vinegar, which we have plenty of in one of our storage rooms here in the farmhouse. But we've got to get that five-gallon drum inside, and that's not going to be possible as long as those insects are out there. They've grown a lot faster and a lot bigger than we thought they would."

"How many of them are there?" Kiersten asked.

"As far as we know," Bill answered, "there are six. When we realized our experiment was getting out of control, we got rid of most of them, while they were still relatively small. Unfortunately, six of them were able to escape by chewing through the fence or simply jumping over it. Now that they're in the wild and have an endless supply of food sources, they're growing faster than ever."

"How big will they get?"

Bill heaved a heavy sigh. "We don't know," he said. "That's something I don't want to think about. What I'd really like to think about is how we're going to stop them, and we won't be able to do that unless my brother can help me. Right now, the only thing we can do is wait until the coast is clear. My brother is pretty smart. He'll wait until all of the crickets are gone, then make a run for the house."

"Bryson will, too," I said.

Bill placed the palms of his hands on the windowsill, leaned forward, and looked outside. "With the five of us working together, I'm sure we can stop the crickets before—"

Bill's words were cut short by an enormous crash from the back of the house. Wood splintered and glass shattered. The floor trembled and shook. At the other end of the hall, I caught a glimpse of an enormous, blue leg.

We were under attack . . . but this time, there was nowhere we could go.

22

It sounded like the entire house was coming down, and as a matter of fact, it was. The giant, blue cricket—by far the biggest of all of them—was crushing the roof and the walls of the farmhouse. I didn't know if it was trying to get at us, or if he simply wanted to demolish the house. Those aren't things you think about when something like this happens. The only thing you think about is staying alive, and that's precisely what I was thinking about at that moment.

But the problem we faced, of course, was

that not only was the blue cricket attacking us from the back of the house, but the giant, green cricket was still out front, near the partially demolished barn. If we fled into the front yard to get away from the blue cricket, there was a very good chance we would be spotted by the green cricket. We already knew how fast they could move, as we'd already had a few close calls. Sooner or later, I knew we weren't going to be so lucky.

But the three of us weren't left with any other choice.

"We've got to try to make it to the cellar!" Bill shouted over the crashing and breaking sounds. "The green cricket is looking the other way. If we hurry, we can make it!"

The sound of destruction thundered in my ears as the blue cricket continued tearing away at the walls and the roof. The horrifying insect was incredibly strong and was tearing through the old farmhouse as if it were made of paper.

Bill opened the front door. "Let's go!" he

shouted. "I'll go first and get the doors to the storm cellar open. Give me a little head start, and then you guys follow. And run as fast as you can!"

I glanced out the window. The colossal, green cricket was still in the driveway near the barn, but he was moving away slowly. Bill was right: if we hurried, there was a chance we could make it to the storm cellar. Then, the five of us would be together. We would be safe, at least for the time being, and we could put together a plan. I felt safer just knowing that Bill and Brad had returned . . . but that didn't mean we were out of danger.

Bill leapt across the porch and raced into the driveway, past the mangled truck heap. In just a few seconds, he was halfway to the storm cellar doors.

"Come on!" I urged Kiersten.

Holding hands, we jumped off the porch and started running. Out of the corner of my eye, I saw the monstrous, green cricket turn toward us, but by then, we were only a few dozen feet away from the storm cellar doors. Bill had already reached the doors and was grasping at the handle.

And here was where we encountered a problem we hadn't thought about. Bryson and Brad had no way of knowing about our plan, and they had not only closed the storm cellar doors, but they had bolted them.

We were locked out.

Bill began pounding on the metal doors.

"Brad!" he yelled. *"Brad! Open up! It's us! Hurry!"*

Suddenly, both metal doors flew open . . . but it was too late. The giant, green cricket had already leapt into the air and was coming down on us!

23

I tried to leap to the right, but I tripped and fell . . . and that's what saved me. By sheer luck, I had landed between two enormous legs. If I hadn't fallen, I probably would have been squished flat.

Kiersten, however, had leapt out of the way, but the insect made a mad grab for her. He missed, but he succeeded in knocking her down. She hit the ground, rolled twice, bounced to her feet, and raced to the waiting storm cellar doors that were being held open by Bill. In the next instant, she vanished.

I, however, wasn't so lucky. My right pant leg was caught under one of the cricket's legs. When I tried to get to my feet, I found that I was stuck.

The only good thing for me was the fact that the insect didn't know I was there. Perhaps the creature was focused on Bill at the storm cellar doors or had been distracted by Kiersten. For whatever reason, its attention wasn't on me.

The cricket lashed out with one of its front legs. Bill ducked beneath the metal door to avoid the sweeping leg. The cricket missed Bill, but succeeded in tearing one of the doors completely from its hinges. It flew through the air and slammed to the ground some forty feet away.

I made one more gigantic effort to tear my pant leg free and succeeded. I didn't think the cricket realized that I was even there, so I remained on the ground, rolling to one side, getting to my hands and knees.

But now I had another problem. The cricket was focused on Bill at the storm cellar. If I went that way, the insect would see me, for sure. The only other option was to run in a different direction.

Nearby was the mangled heap of what was left of the Carpenter brothers' truck, on its side in the driveway. The big white box was broken and damaged, but a hole was torn through the metal and wood. If I could slip through it and get into the box without the creature seeing me, I might have a chance. As long as I remained hidden and the cricket didn't know where I was, he might leave me alone.

Near the entrance of the storm cellar, Bill had backed away, pressed against the wall of the barn. He saw me crawling away and quickly figured out my plan.

"Hurry!" he said. "Hide in the box of the truck! I'll try to distract the cricket so he doesn't see you!"

After crawling frantically on my hands and knees for a few feet, I leapt up and sprinted the rest of the way to the mangled truck. The front cab of the truck was completely smashed flat with broken metal and glass all over the driveway. When I reached the hole in the big box, I squeezed through, being careful not to cut myself on the broken pieces of metal and wood. However, as cautious as I was, I caught my shirt on a sharp piece of jagged steel. I heard the sound of tearing cloth as I continued to wiggle through the hole, but I didn't care. A torn shirt was a small price to pay to get away from the giant beast in the driveway!

Finally, I was all the way inside the mangled box. I didn't have much room, because everything inside had shifted around and tumbled over. I found myself next to the five-gallon drum that Brad had told us about, the container that held the powder that they needed to mix with vinegar to create the powerful insecticide. Other items included some yard tools and two plastic tubes, one yellow and one red, that I recognized as water cannons. I had a similar water gun at home.

Why would the Carpenter brothers have water

cannons? I wondered, but I quickly pushed the thought away. I had more important things to worry about.

I peered out into the driveway. Now that I was hidden, Bill had turned and was running away. Unfortunately for him, the cricket was much, much faster. The insect had no trouble reaching out with one of its right front legs and knocking Bill to the ground, sending him rolling nearly ten feet. Still, Bill jumped to his feet and attempted to flee again.

This time, the insect wasn't playing games. The mammoth beast leaned forward, snapped up Bill with one of its long, powerful legs, and yanked him into the air. Bill struggled and squirmed, but there was no way he was going to be able to free himself.

The insect opened its mouth.

Bill struggled as the cricket brought him closer and closer, opening his mouth even more. He pounded the insect's leg with his fists, but his efforts had no effect on the atrocious cricket.

I closed my eyes and covered my face with my hands, as I couldn't bear to watch what was about to happen.

Bill let out one last, final, painful scream. Then, he fell silent, and the only thing I could hear were horrible crunching sounds . . . .

24

I kept my eyes shut tightly and moved my hands to cover my ears. I couldn't bear listening to the awful crunching sounds as the enormous cricket chewed Bill into tiny bits and pieces.

Then, the chewing stopped. I heard a hissing sound, followed by a squeal. I opened my eyes.

The giant, blue cricket had returned. The crunching sound I had heard wasn't chewing, after all, as I now saw Bill on the ground, running away. The crunching sound came from the blue cricket, who was scraping his two front legs together. The green cricket must have spotted the blue cricket and dropped Bill, and he was no longer interested in the tiny human that was fleeing across the driveway. Instead, his attention was focused on the insect bearing down on him.

Within seconds, the two insects were locked in a fierce battle. Their bodies tumbled to the ground with a thundering crash that shook the earth. They kicked and squealed and clawed at one another.

Suddenly, I didn't feel very safe anymore. I realized that although I was out of sight, I was also trapped. I was stuck in my hiding place, and if one of those crickets, or both of them, rolled over what remained of the box truck, I would be crushed.

I looked around the yard for anywhere else to hide. I might be safe in the house, as it hadn't been totally demolished by the blue cricket, but to get there, I risked being out in the open where I would be in full view of the battling crickets.

But, then again, maybe they were too focused on one another. After all: the green cricket had dropped Bill when he saw the blue cricket coming. Maybe they were less concerned about humans and more concerned with fighting each other. I never knew crickets could be so fierce.

But, then again, these weren't just ordinary crickets. These were colossal monsters, created by an experiment that had gone wrong. Maybe they weren't even real crickets anymore.

No matter. I had to make a decision. The two fighting crickets were rolling on the ground, fiercely battling one another, and they kept getting closer and closer to my hiding spot within the mangled box truck.

Still, I was reluctant to flee. That is, until the two insects made one violent roll and smashed into what was left of the box truck. There was only a small space between the hole in the box and the enormous back of the green cricket. The insect was so close that I could have reached out and touched him!

It was time to make my move. I couldn't wait for the battling insects to roll one more time and crush me within the box truck. I had to act, and fast.

Quickly, I wriggled through the torn wall of the box. There wasn't much room at all, and my escape required me to actually touch the cricket's hard exoskeleton. It grossed me out, but I quickly pushed the thought away. Now wasn't the time to be grossed out by anything. Now was the time to think about getting away, about putting as much distance between me and the crickets as I possibly could.

I squeezed between the box and the cricket, being careful not to catch any of my clothing or cut my skin on the sharp pieces of wood and metal. The entire right side of my body pressed up against the green cricket as I made my escape.

Finally, I made my way around the wreckage of the truck. The old farmhouse wasn't more than thirty feet away, and I wasted no time running as fast as I could across the short driveway. I bounded up the steps, leapt onto the porch, and then burst through the door, slamming it closed behind me. I slumped to the floor with my back pressed against the door, gasping, my lungs heaving for breath.

I made it. I was safe. For how long, I didn't know. All I knew was that I wanted this nightmare to be over. I wanted to be home. I wanted to be anywhere else but the old farmhouse.

But while I was safe inside the house, Kiersten, Bryson, and Brad Carpenter were dealing with their own nightmare in the storm cellar . . . .

25

I sat against the wall for a few minutes, catching my breath. I was so glad I was no longer near those horrible crickets, so glad I was no longer trapped within the mangled wreckage of the box truck.

Still, I knew that we were all in danger. None of us would be safe as long as those crickets were around.

Then, I had an idea.

There must be a phone in the house! I thought. *That's it! I'll call for help!*

I stood, turned, and looked out the window and into the driveway. The two gigantic blue and green crickets were still at one another, locked in fierce battle.

I hurried across the living room and down the hall, but I didn't get far. The blue cricket that had attacked the house had really done a lot of damage, and the rest of the house was impassable. Walls were collapsing, and a portion of the roof had crashed down into the kitchen.

I looked around, but I didn't find a phone.

Bill and Brad must have a phone they carry with them, I thought. *Maybe they'd already called for help. It's not something I can count on, though. Until help arrived—if it ever did—we were all on our own. But if we were smart, we could—*

My thought was interrupted by a noise from the living room, the distinct sound of the front door banging open. Then, it slammed closed.

"Are you in here?" a voice called out.

It was Bill!

I raced back down the hall and burst into

the living room.

"You made it!" I said.

Bill nodded. "I had to circle around to the edge of the woods to keep out of sight," he explained. "Those two big crickets are still fighting in the driveway, so they weren't paying any attention to anything but themselves. There are a couple more still around, though."

"Do you have a phone?" I asked. "If you do, you can call for help."

Again, Bill nodded, but a bit sheepishly this time.

"Brad and I both have phones," he replied, "but they're in the cab of the truck. We didn't have time to grab them before we were attacked. But how about you? Are you okay?"

"Yeah," I replied with a nod. "I'm fine. Kiersten, Bryson, and your brother are in the storm cellar, so I'm sure they are okay, too."

Bill and I looked out the front window, and we both saw something that made me realize I had spoken too soon.

While the two gigantic crickets fought in the driveway, frantically lunging and grasping at one another, another scene was unfolding beyond them.

On the other side of the yard in front of the barn, dark smoke was billowing up into the air . . . *and it was coming from the open doors of the storm cellar!*

26

"Oh, no!" Bill shouted. "There's a fire in the storm cellar!"

"We've got to do something!" I said. "We've got to get Kiersten and Bryson and your brother out of there!"

As if sensing a new danger, the blue and green crickets fighting in the driveway unlocked from one another. With a sudden, huge leap, the blue cricket sprang high into the air and vanished over the trees. Once again, I was amazed at the distance the crickets could leap. One single jump could send them hundreds of feet!

The green cricket righted himself and paused for a moment. He stared at the wisp of smoke billowing out of the storm cellar. Then, he hurried off to the left, passing the barn and crawling his way along the driveway, following the chain-link fence.

It was the chance we needed. I had no idea what was burning in the storm cellar or how it had caught fire, but I knew we had to get Kiersten, Bryson, and Brad out of there, if it wasn't already too late.

Bill and I burst out the front door, bounded across the porch, and tore across the driveway. I turned my head from side to side as we ran, searching for any more of those horrible, giant insects. I didn't see any, but that certainly didn't mean that they weren't around. They might be watching us at that very moment.

Smoke continued to pour out of the open cellar doors. I heard coughing, and it sounded like Kiersten.

Good, I thought. *Maybe we're not too late to get them out.*

I could hear frantic shuffling on the stairs as Bill and I reached the doors. Something moved in the smoke, but I was horrified to find that it wasn't Kiersten.

It wasn't Bryson, and it certainly wasn't Brad.

It was a cricket! The yellow cricket, the one that wasn't as big as the others, was quickly scrambling backward up the steps, making its way out. Bill and I were forced to flee once again. We ran across the driveway to the house and stopped on the porch.

By then, the yellow cricket had emerged from the storm cellar. He took several steps in the driveway, then made a gigantic leap into the air. The effort sent him over the yard and driveway, and he landed within the confines of the fenced-in pasture.

To my great relief, Kiersten emerged from the storm cellar, coughing and sputtering. Bryson was right behind her, followed by Brad Carpenter. All three were carrying rolled-up newspapers that were on fire. They were coughing and gasping for air, but they seemed to be okay. The three dropped the burning newspapers to the ground and stomped out the flames with their feet.

"Over here!" Bill shouted.

Kiersten, Bryson, and Brad turned their heads in our direction, then began sprinting across the driveway, past the mangled truck. All of them were still coughing and hacking, but by the time they reached us on the porch, they had caught their breaths.

"What happened?" Bill asked.

"That cricket crawled down into the storm cellar," Brad replied. "We didn't have anything to defend ourselves with. I grabbed some newspapers, rolled them up, and lit them on fire. The cricket didn't like the flames or the smoke, and we were able to keep him away from us."

"The place filled up with smoke really fast," Bryson said with a cough. "But that was good thinking. It saved our lives."

It was yet another bit of good luck, and I realized we'd been having a string of good fortune. We had been placed in several dangerous situations where we could have lost our lives, but we were all okay. The five of us had survived—so far.

But I also realized that our string of good luck wouldn't last forever, and that sooner or later, it was going to come to an end.

And it was about to . . . much sooner than I expected.

27

"We've got to figure out a way to get that powdered insecticide out of the truck without any crickets seeing us," Brad said. "They know that we're here. They can smell us. They're hungry."

That wasn't a pleasant thought at all. Once again, the image of poor Spaceman popped into my head. I hadn't seen him for a long time, and I hoped that he was safe. Spaceman was very small and would have a better chance of hiding and probably keeping away from the crickets then we did. Still, I worried about him. A lot.

"But what happens if we aren't able to keep away from them?" Bryson asked. "They have to eat. What will they do when they get really super hungry?"

Bill and Brad looked at each other. Their faces showed expressions of deep concern.

"The crickets will eat any living, warm blooded creature," Bill said. "The real problem is that they will grow bigger and bigger the more they eat. Their appetites will increase. They will need more and more food and will move to areas where it will be easier to feed."

He didn't need to explain more. I knew exactly what he was talking about. Sooner or later, if the crickets got hungry enough, they would make their way into the downtown area of Aspen, which was only about a mile away. There, they would find all the food they needed. That food, of course, would be human beings.

It would be disaster on a gigantic scale. I imagined horrified people running and screaming through the downtown district as giant crickets bounded about, crushing buildings and smashing cars, scooping up helpless people as fast as they could. To the giant crickets, humans would be nothing more than an afternoon snack.

"You said you have to mix the insecticide with white vinegar," Kiersten said. "Then, what do you do?"

"We already have the vinegar here in the house," Bill replied. "The insecticide itself, as a powder, isn't dangerous. But when it's mixed with the white vinegar, it becomes a very deadly concoction. Just a very small amount will kill the crickets."

"But how do you get close enough to the crickets?" I asked. "You can't just put this stuff in a glass and throw it at one of them. That would mean you have to get close to them, and they might get you before you get them."

"We've already thought of that," Brad replied. "Do you know what water cannons are?"

"You mean, like, toys?" Bryson asked. "Like those big squirt guns that we play with at the park or at the lake?"

Suddenly, I remembered seeing the two water cannons in the box of the wrecked truck. "There are two of those in the back of your truck!" I said, nearly shouting. "I saw them there while I was hiding!"

Bill nodded. "Our idea was to mix up a batch of the insecticide with the vinegar in a large can. We could use the water cannon to draw out the liquid. Those water cannons can squirt thirty or forty feet, which means we wouldn't have to get that close to the crickets to spray them. Even if an insect came after one of us, the insecticide would kill him instantly."

"Well," I said, "it doesn't look like we have any other choice. We have to get that insecticide from your truck, along with those water cannons, and we have to do it before those crickets head into Aspen."

"And we have to do it without getting killed," Kiersten said.

Again, Brad and Bill looked at each other.

"Before we got here," Bill said, "we thought we could take care of this ourselves. But we had no idea the crickets had grown so big."

"We didn't plan on getting attacked in our truck, either," Brad added. "I never thought such a simple, innocent experiment could go so wrong. But it has, and now we have to do everything we can to fix it. Still, there's only so much that the two of us can do."

"But there's five of us now," I said. "We've got to be able to do something."

"Well," Bill said, "it's going to be dangerous, but you're right: we've got to do something. I don't want to do anything that would put you kids at risk, but the fact is, if we're going to survive, we're going to need your help. And if we all work together, I think we can stop the crickets."

Bryson, Kiersten, and I were silent for a moment. Then, Bryson spoke quietly.

"Do we have any other choice?" he asked.

Brad shook his head. "I'm afraid not."

So, like it or not, the five of us were going to

147

team up in a last ditch effort to stop the crickets and save our lives and, quite possibly, the entire city of Aspen.

The real battle—in every sense a fight to the death—was about to begin.

28

The five of us were quiet for a moment, staring out the kitchen windows. We had a clear view of the fenced-in pasture, the demolished truck, and the three white barns, two of which had been heavily damaged by the giant crickets. Kiersten turned to me with a look of concern on her face.

"Hey," she said, with a troubled frown. "Have you seen your cat?"

I shook my head. "He ran off a while ago. I'm really worried about him. I hope he's okay."

"I don't think the crickets will pay too much

attention to him," Bill said. "Cats aren't very big, and I don't think the crickets are going to be interested in something of that size."

I didn't know if he was saying that just to make me feel better, but he had a point. Spaceman wouldn't make much of a meal for any of those crickets.

Brad looked at me and spoke. "You said you saw the drum with the insecticide inside the truck?" he asked.

I nodded. "Yes," I replied. "I saw it, along with the two water cannons."

"Did it look like they were damaged?"

I shook my head. "Not that I could see," I replied.

"Good," Bill said. "Now is as good a time as any. Let's see if we can retrieve that drum filled with the insecticide and bring it in here."

Bill and Brad discussed this for a few minutes, making plans to figure out how they were going to get the drum out of the truck and into the house. They finally decided that Bill would go first, being that he was smaller. He would scramble into the broken box behind the cab and try to push the five-gallon drum out. Then, Brad would run out and help him, and the two would carry the drum of insecticide to the farmhouse.

"What do you want us to do?" Bryson asked.

"If I'm able to get the drum out of the truck," Bill replied, "I'll toss out the water cannons. If I don't see any of those crickets, I'll yell to you. Which one of you three is fastest?"

Kiersten slowly raised her hand. "I am," she said.

"I'll throw the water cannons as far as I can," Bill said, "so you won't have to go very far to retrieve them. But that will only be if there aren't any crickets around. Understand?"

Kiersten nodded.

"Good," he continued. "When I give you the signal, run out and grab them and bring them back to the house as fast as you can."

"What do you want Kendra and me to do?" Bryson asked.

Brad spoke. "You two stay here at the door and be ready. Bill and I might need help getting the drum inside."

"You know," Bill said, "before we go out there, let's get the white vinegar ready. That way, we'll be able to mix the insecticide right away. There's no telling when or where one of those things is going to show up."

"Good idea," Brad agreed.

The Carpenter brothers strode through the old farmhouse, and we followed them. While the front portion of the house, including the living room and several bedrooms, were fine, the entire back of the house, including the kitchen and a few other rooms, were completely demolished. It was strange to see sunlight streaming into the kitchen where the roof had been torn away.

We came to a bedroom that was empty except for a dozen clear plastic jugs containing a clear liquid. In the corner of the room was a large, empty plastic bucket.

"Let's haul all of these bottles into the living

room," Bill said. "And don't forget to grab the bucket, too."

It didn't take too long to move all the plastic bottles of white vinegar and the bucket into the living room. We opened six of the bottles and poured them into the bucket. The strong odor of white vinegar burned my nostrils. While I wasn't sure how the white vinegar and the insecticide would work together as an agent to kill the crickets, Bill and Brad Carpenter seemed to know what they were doing. I hoped so, anyway, as we were almost out of options.

I was pouring the last bottle of white vinegar into the bucket when I glanced up and looked out the living room window.

And that's when I saw him.

Spaceman. He was sitting at the edge of the driveway not far from the barn and near the edge of the forest, looking around as if he was searching for something.

But I also saw something else.

The yellow cricket.

He was in the woods on the other side of the barn, and the only thing I could see was the insect's head and face, as the rest of his body was concealed behind a mass of branches and leaves.

And it was obvious that Spaceman had no idea the horrific insect was waiting for just the right moment.

Without giving it a second thought, I dropped the empty jug of white vinegar onto the floor, ran across the room, threw open the front door, and bolted outside . . . just as the yellow cricket began crawling toward my cat.

29

I was dimly aware of shouting from behind me, coming from within the old farmhouse. Panicked voices urged me to stop, to come back. I heard my name several times, and I heard Kiersten shriek.

None of that mattered. The only thing that mattered was my cat. Spaceman was in danger. I remembered Brad saying that my cat was probably too small for the insects to care about, but, apparently, that wasn't the case. The yellow cricket was quickly crawling out from the forest, and he was heading right for Spaceman.

Thankfully, Spaceman heard the cracking of branches and brush and was immediately alerted to the danger . He took off running, scampering around one of the partially demolished barns. I had hoped that he would see me and come running up, but he was too frightened. I couldn't blame him.

I skidded to a halt on the hard-packed driveway and quickly turned around, intending to head back to the house. I could still hear the frantic shouts and pleas coming from within the farmhouse. Bill Carpenter stood in the doorway with Kiersten and Bryson next to him. Brad stood in front of the big picture window, looking out.

Kiersten pointed at me and screamed, and I knew there was no way I would make it back to the house in time. Now that Spaceman was gone, the yellow cricket had set his sights on me.

I didn't even take the time to see where the cricket was or how far away he was from me. Instead, I dove toward the smashed truck and quickly scrambled into the crushed box. The opening wasn't big enough for the cricket to get at me, but once again, I realized that I was trapped. If one of the bigger crickets came along and stepped on what was left of the truck, I would be squished like a bug.

And I made it to the safety of the truck just in time. With a crunching thud, the yellow cricket landed next to the demolished vehicle. He poked his front legs into my hiding place, and I had to wiggle and squirm to keep away from them. The long claws at the end of his legs were sharp and curved, and I knew that if he was able to hold onto me, he would be able to very easily pull me out.

After realizing he wasn't going to be able to get me, he withdrew his legs and began to move away. I breathed a sigh of relief as I realized I was pressed up against the large drum filled with the powdered insecticide. While I was certain it was too heavy for me to lift, I wondered if I could roll it forward and perhaps push it through the opening of the box truck.

I rolled around to the other side of the drum

and drew my knees to my chest. I placed my feet against the drum and pushed. It was heavy, but I was able to roll it forward and push it through the jagged opening. It took a lot of effort, but I was able to push it farther away from the cave-like entrance, and it rolled to a stop a couple of feet away.

Then, I rolled back into my cramped hiding place and picked up the red and yellow water cannons. Crawling toward the entrance, I peered outside to see where the yellow cricket was. He had moved away and was crawling along the chain-link fence near the driveway.

I turned and looked at the old farmhouse. Bill, Bryson, and Kiersten were still standing in the doorway with horrified, worried looks on their faces.

Double-checking to make sure there were no other crickets around, I crawled out from my hiding place. Quickly, I bounded to my feet, still carrying the water cannons, and sprinted across the driveway, bounded up the porch, and nearly tripped as I burst through the open front door where my friends were waiting.

"That was a close call!" Bryson said.

"But you got the water cannons!" Kiersten said, excitedly.

Brad had been standing by the living room window, and he strode to the door and stood next to his brother.

"Great work," he said. "Now, all we have to do is get that drum filled with the insecticide into the house."

The five of us turned and looked outside. The yellow cricket had vanished into the woods, and there was no sign of any of the other crickets.

Which was, of course, good news and bad news. It was good news because none of them were around to threaten us. But it was bad news because maybe the crickets had already decided that we weren't worth the effort. Maybe they had moved on. Maybe they were already wandering the streets of Aspen, creating madness and mayhem.

"Let's go," Bill said. "We can't waste any more time."

Bill and Brad hustled outside the house and raced across the driveway. It took them only a few seconds to reach the large drum laying sideways on the ground.

A huge shadow suddenly fell over the entire house, the demolished truck, the driveway, and the barns. It was as if a fast-moving cloud suddenly blotted out the sun.

If only that were the case.

No, what created the shadow was no cloud. It was the enormous, green cricket. Where he had been, I didn't know. But he had taken a gigantic leap and was now coming down out of the sky, faster and faster, and was going to land right on top of Bill and Brad Carpenter!

30

The sweeping shadow alerted Bill and Brad to the danger, and they both looked up at the same time. Brad darted to the left while Bill ran to the right, past the demolished truck. Bill dove to the ground and rolled just as the cricket crashed to the ground. One of his legs landed on what was left of the box truck and completely crushed it, flat as a napkin. If I had been there, hiding inside, I would never have made it out alive.

The enormous cricket sat in the driveway for a moment, standing as tall as the surrounding trees. His head cocked curiously to the left, then to the right, then back to the left, as if he was deciding which direction to go, who he was going to pursue. Right in front of him, on the ground, sat the drum of insecticide. Thankfully, the insect hadn't stepped on it. I was sure that if he had, it would've broken open. Then, the powder would have spilled harmlessly in the driveway, erasing our chances of victory.

Both Bill and Brad had vanished. Brad ran into the woods, while Bill slipped around the side of the farmhouse.

The giant, green cricket began moving slowly to our left, where he easily crushed the fence beneath his powerful legs. He didn't appear to be in a hurry, nor did he appear to be going after Bill or Brad.

"Let's see if we can get the insecticide into the house," I whispered.

"Are you crazy?" Kiersten hissed.

"No," I answered back, shaking my head. "We can't wait. If we do, more of those crickets

162

might show up. We have to find a way to defend ourselves."

"We need to wait for Bill and Brad to come back," Bryson said.

Again, I shook my head. "We can't count on them coming back," I said. "The only chance we have is to do this on our own."

"But we have no idea what to do," Kiersten said.

"Bill and Brad said all they had to do was mix the powdered insecticide with the white vinegar," I said. "That's all we have to do. We've already got the water cannons. All we need to do is roll that drum filled with insecticide into the house, get it open, mix the powder with the white vinegar, and fill the water cannons. Then, we'll be able to defend ourselves."

We remained silent for a moment, thinking about what we were up against, what was at stake. Then, Bryson spoke.

"Kendra's right," he said. "If we don't act on our own, if we don't do something quick, those

163

things are going to get us. We've already seen how easily they can demolish the house. So far, we've been lucky that one of those things hasn't destroyed the rest of this place."

We watched as the enormous, green cricket continued his way through the pasture. When he made it to the other side, he broke through the chain-link fence as if it were paper. Then, he entered the woods, snapping tree trunks and branches as he went.

"Let's go," I said, giving one last look around the yard and the forest to make sure no other crickets were nearby.

The three of us raced out the door, over the porch, and across the driveway. A quick movement caught my attention—something small. It came out from the side of one of the demolished barns and began scampering toward us.

"Spaceman!" I shouted as my cat raced toward me. I was thankful that he was still safe and alive, but I had to stay focused on our present task.

Bryson, Kiersten, and I ran to the other side of the drum. Placing our hands on the smooth surface, we began pushing, rolling the drum across the driveway. It was heavy, but we managed, and the harder we pushed, the faster the drum began to roll until it smacked into the first step of the wooden porch.

"We're going to have to try to lift it," I said as the three of us repositioned ourselves around the drum. We grunted and struggled, but we were finally able to raise it up over the steps and onto the porch, where we began rolling it toward the door. It took a lot of effort, but we were finally able to get it through the doorway and into the living room, where we stood it up.

"Let's get the lid off!" I said.

The lid was made of hard plastic, and it was sealed tight. Bryson, however, was able to get his fingertips beneath the edge and work the lid up. Within seconds, he had removed the lid and tossed it to the side.

The insecticide was a creamy white powder.

It had no smell.

"Don't touch it," I said. "We need to find something to scoop it out and put it in the bucket of white vinegar."

Bryson raced around the drum and into the living room and then hurried to the demolished kitchen. We heard clanging and banging, and then:

"Got it!" he said, and he quickly returned with a plastic bowl.

"Hurry!" Kiersten said as she glanced nervously out the living room window.

Bryson carefully scooped up a bowl full of insecticide and rushed to the waiting bucket of white vinegar. Then, he cautiously poured the powder into the liquid.

"How much of that powder should we add?" he asked.

I shrugged. "I have no idea," I replied. "But you'd better add some more, just in case."

Bryson returned to the drum of insecticide several times, pouring bowl after bowl into the bucket.

I picked up the red water cannon and used the barrel to stir the poisonous concoction in the bucket. Then, with the barrel immersed in the liquid, I drew the handle back, creating a vacuum. The liquid insecticide began filling the plastic barrel. Kiersten picked up the yellow water cannon and began to do the same.

And that's when the roof came down on us.

31

The three of us were knocked violently to the floor. I dropped the red water cannon that I was holding, but at the moment, I wasn't aware of it. The only thing I was aware of was that beams and boards had come down upon me. I wasn't hurt, but I was certainly surprised, shocked, and scared.

I heard Kiersten shriek and Bryson scream. Immediately, I began pushing boards away from me and found I was able to stand. Seeing the water cannon at my feet, I bent over and snapped it up.

Thankfully, Bryson and Kiersten weren't injured, either. They, too, frantically pushed the wooden beams away and stood.

A portion of the wall and part of the ceiling had caved in, and we quickly saw the reason why.

The monster, blue cricket had landed next to the house. One of his legs had hit the roof and punctured it, collapsing a portion of the ceiling and shattering a bearing wall. Currently, a gigantic, blue leg filled part of the living room, but the insect hadn't spotted us.

Yet.

Wordlessly, I waved to get Bryson and Kiersten's attention, then silently pointed toward the hall. If we were quiet, perhaps the cricket wouldn't even know that we were there.

Cautiously, I stepped over and around pieces of broken wood, drywall, and foam insulation, making my way through the living room and into the hallway. It was simply unbelievable how much destruction had occurred so quickly. Because of their massive size, the crickets were capable of devastation on a massive scale.

Kiersten and Bryson followed close behind me. As soon as we made it to the hall, the cricket moved its leg, knocking over another portion of the wall, sending debris and broken pieces of the house flying. At first, I thought the insect was going to move away, off in another direction. Instead, another leg appeared, destroying even more of the house. Wood snapped and glass shattered.

But I still had the water cannon filled with the poisonous concoction. I raised up the weapon, held it at my hip, and aimed the barrel at the insect's legs. Kiersten did the same, leveling her water cannon at the giant bug, ready to push the handle forward and release a deadly spray of the liquid insecticide.

"Ready?" I whispered.

Kiersten nodded. "As ready as I'll ever be," she replied quietly.

I took a breath, and hoping for the best, I forced the water cannon's handle forward as hard as I could. Immediately, the deadly insecticide spewed forth in a huge, liquid blast. It connected quickly, soaking the cricket's leg that was in the living room.

Kiersten's aim was just as good, and the blast from her water cannon also soaked the creature's leg.

"You got him!" Bryson said triumphantly, but his last word was cut off by an unearthly, terrible sound. It was a horrible, piercing wailing, so loud that I wanted to cup my hands over my ears. In fact, that's precisely what Bryson did. I would have, but that would have meant I had to drop my water cannon, and it was still half full of the poisonous insecticide. I was sure I was going to need it, and I wanted to keep it at the ready.

In the living room, the cricket's leg made a violent forceful move that knocked down the rest of the far wall, exposing open air and daylight. He stopped wailing and froze.

For a moment, I didn't think the insecticide had worked. Bill and Brad Carpenter had told us that it would kill the bugs on contact, but this cricket was still alive. He was still standing partially in the living room.

"It's not working!" Kiersten said. She sounded panicked and frightened, and I started looking around, planning to flee. If the insecticide wasn't going to work, we'd probably done nothing more than make the cricket angry, and we would have to figure out another plan. That is, of course, if we would be able to escape its clutches.

"Wait a minute," Bryson said. "Something's happening."

I held my breath and waited.

I watched.

Kiersten watched.

Bryson watched.

The cricket attempted to move one of his legs, but he stumbled, as if he was unsure of himself. By now, we could see the entire creature looming above us. The house was a complete disaster, in shambles.

"It's working!" Kiersten exclaimed. "It's

really, really working!"

Kiersten was right. The cricket appeared to be unsteady and unsure of himself.

And then, the insect began to collapse, leaning to the side. He was falling over.

But he was falling over . . . right on top of the three of us!

32

The only direction we could go was down the hall, in the opposite direction, and it was littered with debris. The three of us turned and sprang at the same time. Kiersten almost knocked Bryson off his feet, but he recovered and was able to stay afoot, leaping over broken boards and beams.

"Hurry! Hurry! Hurry!" I screamed. I could hear snapping and loud crunching sounds as the dying cricket began to collapse into the house.

We managed to make it to the end of the hall, which turned out to be a dead end. The only escape route was through a bedroom, but it was blocked by a large chunk of the roof that had caved in. I spun—just in time to see the gigantic cricket tumble headlong into the house with an enormous crash. Dust and debris swelled up all around us. Several shingles snapped off the roof and bounced off my shoulders, but they didn't hurt, and I hardly noticed them. I was too busy trying to catch my breath as I looked at the giant, blue insect that now lay dead within the remains of the demolished old farmhouse.

For the moment, we didn't say anything. We just stood there at the end of the hall among the debris, gasping for air, still horrified by what had just happened, but awestruck by the sheer size of the gigantic cricket. Finally, Kiersten broke the silence and spoke.

"Right now," she began, "we are three of the luckiest kids on the planet."

"Not yet," Bryson said. "We won't be three of the luckiest kids on the planet until we make it home alive."

Bryson was right. While we had been lucky in killing the giant cricket, there were still more of them out there. We could be attacked again at any moment.

We heard a shout in the distance; it was Bill or Brad, but I couldn't tell which one.

"We're here!" I shouted back. "We're in the house! We're okay!"

Pushing away pieces of the demolished house, I made my way back through the hallway. Bryson and Kiersten followed. Several times, I was forced to brush up against the giant dead cricket, and each time I did, I cringed. If we made it out alive, I knew that I would never look at another cricket without thinking of this awful day.

Finally, we made it to what was left of the living room. The entire front of the house was gone, fully exposed to the open air. In the driveway, Bill and Brad were rushing toward us.

"Are you guys okay!?!?" Bill asked as the three of us stepped over even more debris and onto the porch.

Kiersten and I were still carrying the water cannons, and we held them up.

"We killed the blue one!" she said proudly. "The insecticide worked!"

"I was pretty sure it would," Bill responded as he looked at the motionless cricket laying in the remains of the farmhouse. He held out his hands, and I handed the water cannon to him.

"We mixed up a bucket full of the stuff," I said, pointing to the wreckage in the living room. I spotted the bucket. Miraculously, it was standing upright and hadn't been knocked over when the cricket came crashing down.

"Now what?" Bryson said as Kiersten handed her water cannon to Brad.

"We load these things up again and get you guys out of here, that's what," Brad said. "We can handle them on our own, but it's going to be too dangerous for you three to hang out around here. But I sure am glad you were able to get that insecticide out of the truck and mix up a batch with the white vinegar. You guys are heroes."

I didn't feel like a hero. I didn't feel like a hero at all. I just felt lucky to be alive and to be able to have a great story to tell.

But we still would have to make it home . . . and that turned out to be a bit trickier than I thought.

33

The plan sounded simple: Bill and Brad, armed with water cannons filled with their special insecticide, were going to escort us home. They would be at our side while we followed the trail. That way, if any crickets showed up, they could take care of them.

"But what if they all attack at the same time?" Bryson asked.

Bill shook his head. "I don't think that will happen," he said. "There are only five of them left, and I think they're scattered throughout the woods."

"We can talk while we walk," Brad said. "The faster we get you guys home, the faster we can begin hunting down the rest of those crickets."

I was all in favor of that! I love the woods, but at that moment, I wanted to be anywhere else. I wanted to be somewhere safe.

Kiersten was able to retrieve her bike, but Bryson's bike was gone, as it had been eaten by the giant, blue cricket.

"I'm real sorry about that," Brad said as we passed the spot where the insect had chewed the bicycle. There were several broken spokes on the ground and part of a chain, but that was it.

"We'll buy you a new one and have it delivered to your house," Bill said. "It was our fault that this whole thing got out of hand. Buying you a new bike is the least we can do."

"I'm just glad to be alive," Bryson said. I don't know how many times I had thought that same thing.

Kiersten picked up her bike, which had been

spared by the crickets. Maybe they didn't like the color. She pushed it while we walked. Bill and Brad kept apologizing to us, telling us that they were done with their experiments, that they were just going to continue farming crickets in Louisiana, just like they had in the past.

I sure was glad to hear that!

We were about halfway home, still following the trail, when we heard a noise in the woods. Something big and heavy. The five of us stopped and peered around, looking into the forest around us. Bill and Brad were standing on either side of the three of us, water cannons raised, ready for anything.

Well, almost anything. They were searching the shadowy forest, looking for any sign of a cricket, but that's not where the insect was. The insect had sprung into the air, and in the next second, he appeared above us in the sky . . . and he was going to land directly on top of us!

34

The five of us scattered, just in the nick of time. The huge, black cricket came crashing down right in the middle of the trail. We escaped uninjured by leaping out of the way, but the giant insect crushed Kiersten's bicycle.

We all had tumbled to the ground, but Brad and Bill had been prepared. Both of them rolled, leapt to their feet, and faced the cricket.

"I'll get him!" Brad shouted, and he pumped the handle of his water cannon halfway. A spray of insecticide spewed forth, covering the giant black cricket. Instantly, the insect fell to the trail, dead.

Bryson, Kiersten, and I got to our feet. Bill and Brad looked at the dead insect, then at us.

"Looks like you get a new bike, too," Bill said to Kiersten.

When we finally reached the end of the trail, which ended at our subdivision, the five of us stopped. And then Spaceman appeared from out of the bushes on the side of the trail. He must have been following us this whole time, hiding along the trail from the crickets. I was really glad he was home safely with us.

Bill pulled a pen and a business card from his pocket and asked Bryson and Kiersten for their addresses, so he could have their new bikes delivered to them. They offered to pay for my torn shirt, but I told them no, that it was an old shirt, anyway.

"Besides," I said, inspecting the tear in the cloth. "I'd like to keep it as a souvenir."

And that's how Kiersten, Bryson, and I saved Aspen from being invaded by giant, carnivorous crickets. As you can imagine, nobody believed us. Everyone wanted proof and wanted to see the dead crickets. We told them we weren't going anywhere near the forest or the old, destroyed farmhouse ever again. A year later, I heard the farmhouse and the property had been bought by a family, and they'd rebuilt the home and were living there. So, I figured we'd seen the last of those awful crickets.

And I couldn't have been happier.

When school began in the fall, there was a new kid in class. His family moved from Salt Lake City, Utah, and they were the ones who had bought the farmhouse that had been demolished by the crickets. His name was Tony Grosset, and he sat in the chair to the right of me. During lunch, I talked to him some more, and I told him about the crickets that the Carpenter brothers had grown, and how their experiment had gotten way out of hand. I was surprised when he said he believed me! He said that the old owners, Bill and Brad Carpenter, had told his parents everything that happened, but they didn't believe him.

"So," I said, "if your parents don't believe the Carpenter brothers, how come *you* do?"

"Because of something that happened to me over the summer in Utah," Tony replied.

"What happened to you?" I said, taking a bite of my peanut butter and jelly sandwich.

"I was attacked by zombies," Tony replied, very matter-of-factly.

I laughed so hard I nearly choked on my sandwich.

"Go ahead and laugh," Tony said. "But it really happened."

I was struck by his sincerity. Somehow, I knew he wasn't lying.

"You're serious?" I said.

Tony nodded.

"You've got to tell me!" I said, taking another bite of my sandwich.

Tony looked at the clock. "I guess I have time to tell you about it before we head back to class," he said. "It all started one day when a friend of mine and I went to hunt for fossils . . . ."

Tony continued talking, and I listened intently, mesmerized by one of the most horrifying zombie stories I had ever heard.

Next:

#37: The Underground Undead of Utah

Continue on for a FREE preview!

1

"Tony, have you finished cleaning your room?" my mom called out from the kitchen. Then, I heard her footsteps coming down the hall.

Rats.

I quickly shoved my comic book under my pillow and leapt off my bed just as Mom appeared in the doorway. She looked around my room, dismayed.

"Have you done anything at all?" she said, placing her hands on her hips.

"I'm just getting things organized," I replied.

"You know . . . just thinking about where everything should go."

"Well, you'd better get a move on and get this room picked up," Mom said, "or else you're not going with your friends this afternoon. And I don't want you throwing things in your closet or under your bed like you did last month."

"Okay," I said sheepishly.

Mom left, and I looked around my room. It really *was* messy. There was a stack of comic books on my dresser, a pile of dirty clothing in the corner, a pile of clean clothing at the foot of my bed, a bunch of books on the floor . . . I didn't even know where to begin. And my closet was packed with so many things I was afraid to open the door!

But, if I didn't get my bedroom cleaned up, I wouldn't get to go fossil hunting with Seth and Savannah Nelson, my best friends from across the street. We'd been planning on hiking the foothills of the mountains behind our house to look for fossils in a small rock quarry not far away. A few days ago I'd found a fossil of a trilobite, which is a type of small marine animal that existed over 250 million years ago! When I showed it to Seth and Savannah, they became just as excited as I was. They wanted to go hunt for fossils with me, so we'd made plans to go later today . . . if, of course, I got my room cleaned up. But so far, I'd done nothing but sit on my bed and read comic books.

I worked furiously for the next hour, putting my clothing in my dresser and on hangers in the closet. I rearranged the books and comics on my bookshelf, and made sure that I cleaned under my bed. I even cleaned out my closet. There were a few things I didn't want anymore, so I put them in a box to take to the thrift store. I swept the floor, and even dusted my desk and chair.

Finally, I was finished, and I had to admit: I was quite pleased with myself. It was the best my room has looked in a long time.

Even Mom was impressed.

"You did a great job," she said. "This is how your room is supposed to look. Let's see how long you can keep it this way."

Cool, I thought. *Now I get to go fossil hunting with Seth and Savannah. Maybe we'll find something really awesome, like dinosaur bones!*

Well, we wouldn't find any dinosaur bones that afternoon, but we'd make an incredible discovery, all right. As a matter of fact, what we were going to find was more shocking and horrifying that I could ever imagine.

2

My family lives in Farmington, Utah. I don't think many people have heard of Farmington, but it's a small city just north of Salt Lake City, and I think most people have heard of that. Both of my parents work in Salt Lake City, and my grandparents live there.

Farmington is really cool. We live on the outskirts east of town, and we can see the foothills of the mountains outside our windows. When I'm not reading or playing video games, I'll spend hours hiking around, hunting for rocks and fossils.

That's how I discovered the trilobite fossil. I'd found a small, rocky area in the side of a steep hill about a mile from home. There were no houses nearby, nothing but trees and hills and rocks of all sizes. Seth, Savannah and I were going to return to that same place to see if there was anything else we could find.

It was Saturday. Dad was playing golf, and Mom was working in her garden while keeping an eye on my little brother, Marshall. He's only two years old, and he's pretty cute. But he's always getting in to things, so you have to really watch him carefully.

I slid open the glass door and stepped out onto our back porch.

"I'm going over to the Nelson's," I called out to Mom. "Then, Seth and Savannah and I are going fossil hunting."

Mom was kneeling next to a row of colorful flowers, and she looked up at me, squinting in the late morning sun. "Make sure you take some water with you," she replied. "It's going to be a hot one today."

That was a good idea. I went back inside, found my aluminum water bottle, and filled it from the faucet in the kitchen. Then, I put it in my backpack and slipped it over one shoulder.

I went out the front door, hurried across the lawn, and crossed the street. Seth and Savannah live directly across from our house. They are twins and look very much alike, except that Seth is a boy and Savannah is a girl. They both have blonde hair, but Seth's is cut short, while Savannah's hair is long.

I had just leapt over the curb when I heard a strange moan that caused me to stop.

I turned my head, unable to comprehend what I was seeing.

On the sidewalk, not far away, was a zombie . . . *and he was coming toward me!*

3

Although it was a hot day, a sudden chill iced down my spine. I nearly dropped my backpack.

On the sidewalk, stumbling toward me, was a boy about my age, except for the fact that he looked like a zombie! There were dark circles around his eyes, and the skin on his face appeared to be falling off.

I wanted to run, but my legs wouldn't move. I had been reading a zombie comic book that very morning, and now I was looking at a real, live zombie!

Or, rather, a real *dead* zombie, being that zombies aren't alive.

But zombies aren't supposed to be *real,* either. They're just make-believe, created by writers for books and movies.

Suddenly, the zombie stopped and spoke to me.

"Whaddya think, Tony?"

I recognized the voice. "Andrew? Is that you?" I asked.

"Yeah," he replied. "I bought this zombie costume at a garage sale for a dollar. I know it's not Halloween, but I couldn't wait to try it out."

I grinned. Andrew Norton lived a couple of blocks over. Last year, we'd been in the same classroom.

"You sure freaked me out for a minute," I said.

"That's the idea," Andrew replied. "I've already freaked out a few people this morning. I'll see you later."

"See ya," I replied as Andrew continued his

fake stumbling movements. He really did look like a zombie, and I imagined that he would probably scare more than a few people before he was done.

I strode up to the Nelson's house and rang the doorbell. Mrs. Nelson came to the door. She has blonde hair like Savannah, except it's not as long.

"Hello, Tony," she said. "Looking for Seth and Savannah?"

"Yeah," I replied.

"They're in the backyard. I think they're waiting for you."

I walked around the side of the house and found Seth and Savannah, tossing a Frisbee back and forth to one another. When Seth saw me, he threw the disc in my direction. I dropped my backpack to the ground, leapt up into the air, caught the Frisbee, and launched it back at Savannah. She snatched it out of the air and flung it back to Seth.

"Ready to find some fossils?" I said as Seth tossed the Frisbee to me. The disc sailed over my head, and I had to run to catch it.

"I am!" Savannah said.

"Me, too!" Seth said. "I want to find something cool, like that trilobite you found a couple of days ago."

I tossed the Frisbee to Savannah and picked up my backpack. She caught it, and the three of us converged in the backyard.

"What's in the backpack?" Seth asked.

"Just a bottle of water," I said. "I wanted to bring my pack just in case we find a lot of fossils."

"Good thinking," Seth said. "We'll get some water, too."

I followed Seth and Savannah into their house, and waited while they retrieved their water bottles and filled them up at the kitchen sink.

Five minutes later, we'd crossed the street and were heading across the field behind our house, each of us carrying our own backpack, on our way to the foothills. Everything about the day was perfect: a perfect blue sky, perfect warm weather, a perfect cool breeze.

And I was with my two best friends. The three of us were excited, hoping to find some fossils.

Everything was *perfect*.

Not for long.

ABOUT THE AUTHOR

Johnathan Rand has been called 'one of the most prolific authors of the century.' He has authored more than 75 books since the year 2000, with well over 4 million copies in print. His series include the incredibly popular **AMERICAN CHILLERS, MICHIGAN CHILLERS, FREDDIE FERNORTNER, FEARLESS FIRST GRADER,** and **THE ADVENTURE CLUB.** He's also co-authored a novel for teens (with Christopher Knight) entitled **PANDEMIA.** When not traveling, Rand lives in northern Michigan with his wife and three dogs. He is also the only author in the world to have a store that sells only his works: **CHILLERMANIA!** is located in Indian River, Michigan and is open year round. Johnathan Rand is not always at the store, but he has been known to drop by frequently. Find out more at:

www.americanchillers.com

ATTENTION YOUNG AUTHORS!
DON'T MISS

JOHNATHAN RAND'S

AUTHOR QUEST®

THE DEFINITIVE WRITER'S CAMP
FOR SERIOUS YOUNG WRITERS©

If you want to sharpen your writing skills, become a better writer, and have a blast, Johnathan Rand's Author Quest is for you!

Designed exclusively for young writers, Author Quest is 4 days/3 nights of writing courses, instruction, and classes in the secluded wilds of northern lower Michigan. Oh, there are lots of other fun indoor and outdoor activities, too . . . but the main focus of Author Quest is about becoming an even better writer! Instructors include published authors and (of course!) Johnathan Rand. No matter what kind of writing you enjoy: fiction, non-fiction, fantasy, thriller/horror, humor, mystery, history . . . this camp is designed for writers who have this in common: they LOVE to write, and they want to improve their skills!

For complete details and an application, visit:

www.americanchillers.com

Johnathan Rand travels internationally for school visits and book signings! For booking information, call:

1 (231) 238-0338!

www.americanchillers.com

All AudioCraft books are proudly printed, bound, and manufactured in the United States of America, utilizing American resources, labor, and materials.

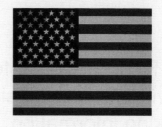

USA